Science Fiction Fantasies, Tales and Origins

Bill Eckel

Published by Bill Eckel, 2023.

Also by Bill Eckel

Shem's Quest
Shem o' the West

Standalone
Hard Kill
Science Fiction Fantasies, Tales and Origins

Watch for more at https://www.billeckel.com.

Table of Contents

Dedication

Each time I publish a book, I realize how many moving parts there are and how many people it takes to put these parts together in a presentable fashion. With each book I strive to present to the reader a better story than I did before. These things I do, I do for you. Thank you.

Acknowledgements

I'd like to thank Pat at Edit Alley for all her help and wisdom. Also, the talented artists at Deranged Doctor Design for the cover.
And, of course, Dana, without whom I wouldn't have begun to know where to start researching.

Shameless plug:
Billeckel.com
Editalley.com
Derangeddoctordesign.com

The Cyborg Rebellion

It was a bitch getting thrown off Earth. Not that I would go back if I could. As Transhumanists, or h+ers as the judge and jury derisively called us, we had worn out our welcome.

The same could be said about the Fleshie — natural human — rock drillers I watched on my wi-fi implant monitoring the security feeds. The Fleshie presence, witnesses to the execution of their foreman by mech overseers, had escalated into a rescue attempt.

I pushed away from my desk in the Security ready room I shared with Alpha Detachment. The three squad leaders looked in my direction, ready to spring into action. They turned away as I leaned back in my chair, resting my heels on an open drawer. I figured I may as well get comfortable as I assessed the situation. Lord knows the rough-hewn tunnels and rooms beneath the surface of Eris, our new paradise, provided little enough comfort.

The way I saw it, there was no hurry. How much damage could some dozen-and-a-half rock drillers do to three Petronovich Mark IIs, and when you got down to it, who cared?

A chirping alarm from my brain chip interrupted the security feed. Bertrand D'Arcy, leader of Eris and head of the Royal Council, demanded my attention. I gave it. "Counts Palatine."

"General Urakurtz, what the hell's going on at the Holding Cells? Why were Fleshies allowed to bring hand-held lasers?"

"Apparently, the Fleshies disagree with the Council's decision to let mechs push them out of Justice Lock."

"You're the Chief of Security, do something about it."

"I'm on it."

Rising from my chair, I kicked the drawer shut. Heads turned at the sudden clang. I grabbed my whiner, an SR-2 standard issue sonic rifle, and ordered, "Charlie Squad, fall in. We got Fleshies attacking mechs at Justice Lock.

Charlie Squad erupted into motion, grabbing their whiners from the ready racks and adjusting the collapsible helmets worn like a torq around their necks. The helmets were required equipment for all Fleshies, civilian or otherwise, living or working on First Level.

The Squad leader bitched, "Christ, I fucking knew it."

So did I. I wanted to sympathize with the Squad leader. It was well-known but of little concern to the Royal Council, that Fleshies resented their mech overseers. Hell, I resented the council's mechs, especially when council member Knyaz Dmitri Petronovich insisted I upload into one. As if I would trade my pretty face and chiseled pecs for one of his nano-skinned robotic copies, no matter how human it looked.

While it was required of Council members to have at least one neural implant for communications, I had long ago chosen longevity drugs as my path to immortality and I had no desire to change my mind. I also had no desire to fight the rock drillers. Unfortunately, as Chief of Security on this god-forsaken rock, I could not allow a disruption of the Royal Council's decree.

Pounding footfalls echoed off the tunnel walls as I led Charlie Squad to Justice Lock.

Fleshies had proved problematic for the Council since arriving on Eris. They had an attitude and bred like rabbits. They were tolerated only because we transhumanists considered manual labor beneath us. Elitists don't live by the sweat of their brows. Early on, the Royal Council devised a method of control. Justice Lock.

Like the Tower of London on old Earth, Justice Lock was the last stop for the growing number of human malcontents. Witnessed by their peers, Fleshies entered the lock from First Level and a Fleshie from Eridian Security pushed them into the vacuum of space. Problem solved.

Today, for the first time, a *mech* would push a Fleshie out of the lock. I had argued against the change, but Dmitri had insisted. The Council sided with the Knyaz.

I burst through the door of the Holding Cells, Charlie Squad hard on my heels. Before us swirled a melee. The acrid smell of burnt positronic fluid, blood, and death stung my nostrils. I surveyed the scene.

One of the Mark IIs brought his fist down upon the head of the driller foreman, crushing the human's skull. The foreman, hands bound behind his back, collapsed to the ground, his head leaking gray matter.

Laser beams focused on the mech. Arms, legs, and smoking lased-out sections of his torso clanked to the deck next to the foreman. The pieces joined the five dead Fleshies and other cut-up mechanical body parts of a Mark II already on the tunnel floor.

Amid the carnage, the last mech stood on the edge of the metal frame that anchored the lock to the rock of Eris. The mech's back butted up to the entrance of Justice Lock. The Fleshies concentrated their fire at it, burning away the skin, exposing white-hot bare metal that wouldn't last much longer. That it had yet to succumb indicated the newness of the model. With the foreman already dead, I decided to put an end to the festivities. Enough Fleshies had died for one day.

I motioned. Charlie squad fanned out on each side of me, whiners leveled. I called out, "Eridian Security. Cease fire."

One of the Fleshies broke away from the group. Two steps took him to the control panel of Justice Lock. He slammed his hand down on the lock activator. With an audible clank of finality, the securing clamps released. The outer door of the air lock slowly slid open. Air escaping into the vacuum of space formed a suction.

My collapsible helmet activated as did the claw-like rock grippers lining the soles of my boots. Dead Fleshies and robotic parts slid toward the air lock. The surviving mech, anchored by the magnetic soles of his feet, refused to disengage. He struggled toward the cluster of Fleshies desperately clinging to the foot anchors sprinkled throughout the floor of the foyer. A few Fleshies, finding neither anchors nor the grasping hands of their companions, were sucked toward the lock and the mech.

I growled. "Well, shit."

This group of Fleshies might have been willing to sacrifice themselves, but I had no desire to join them. Using the implanted wi-fi integrator embedded in my brain chip. I entered the Central Computer and overrode the Justice Lock control panel. The outer lock reversed direction. With the narrowing of the opening, the roar of escaping atmosphere increased, while the strength of the suction decreased.

"Charlie Squad, mute your speakers."

I adjusted my whiner and fired an aural grenade over the heads of the rock drillers. The ear-piercing explosion, amplified by the speakers in their helmets, stunned the Fleshies. Most heaved the contents of their stomachs. The semi digested remains of their last meal filled the lower half of their helmets.

I shifted my attention to the surviving mech. Once clear of the lock's metal framework, it slid back a step for every one it took forward. Still, it attempted to reach the Fleshies.

I shook my head. *What a diehard bastard.* Not that I thought a machine deserved a human attribute, even a derogatory one. I grunted and set my rifle to lethal and fired again.

Cocooned in a laser beam, the super-agitated sound wave easily cut through the mech's metal framework. The head and chest, sucked into the lock, wedged in the outer door. Like a death wail, a screeching of metal-on-metal assaulted my ears. I shivered in terror. Others clasped their hands to the sides of their helmets. Finally, space claimed the last victim of this encounter and the door closed.

My helmet collapsed back into the torq. The grippers released my feet. Satisfied that I had the situation under control, I faced the Fleshies. At two meters and a hundred and nine kilograms, I was an imposing figure.

My voice boomed with authority and fury. "You know who I am." I pointed. "Look at the screen."

The screen above the lock showed the detritus of the fight floating in space. Fleshies grumbled. Charlie Squad leveled their weapons at the Fleshies. The grumbling ceased.

"Justice is served." I said, "Pick up your weapons and go home."

"We'll not be put to death by mechs," spat a spokesman. "We'll not!"

I ignored him. "Squad leader, post two men."

Two men positioned themselves in front of the lock controls. Not particularly wanting to shoot anyone else, I shouldered my whiner and took out my knife. I drew it across my left palm and held it up for all to see. Blood trickled out of the cut and dripped to the deck. "We're all Fleshies here," I said. "We all bleed."

That seemed to calm them, somewhat. I hefted my whiner and pointed it in the direction of Justice Lock. "Now, unless you want to breathe vacuum, you'll go home. I'll carry your words to the Royal council."

The Fleshies filed out of the Holding Cells, all except the spokesman. He looked at the blood still dripping from my palm. He offered his hand. "Thanks."

I looked at his hand. It meant nothing to me. My job description did not require me to like those I protected. I shifted my gaze to his eyes. "For what?"

"For listening. For taking our words to the Royals," he said.

I had no intention of being a hero to the Fleshies and resented being put in the position of appearing that way. I spoke in a flat monotone. "We all live on this rock. We need to get along."

The spokesman withdrew his hand. "We'll meet again, Kwami Urakurtz. One day even the big, black, ex-general of the Planetary Peacekeepers will need help."

The spokesman left the Holding Cells.

I muttered under my breath, "Damn you, Dmitri."

Unlike most transhumanists, I didn't hate Fleshies. I just wanted to live forever. Granted, I had wanted to do that on Earth, but that starship left the landing pad. Eris was home, and I would make the best of it. It would be a lot easier if Dmitri didn't constantly fan the flames, but you can't tell a Royal a damn thing. The Knyaz listened to *one* voice and it damn sure didn't belong to his cousin, Bertrand D'Arcy. Nor did it belong to me.

My implant chirped an incoming message. I answered. "Counts Palatine."

"Report to the council chambers immediately."

The interface terminated abruptly.

The meeting had begun by the time I arrived at the council chambers aboard Station 1, the space station that harbored Eris' government until the Fleshies completed converting the planet below into paradise. I heard the banging of the gavel as soon as the pneumatic doors whisked opened.

Dmitri must have irritated Bertrand. Raised to rule by autocratic elites, Bertrand rarely showed emotion, but the gavel gave him away. He really hammered it when frustrated. Catching my eye, he set it down on the table within easy reach.

As Counts Palatine, Bertrand sat at the head of a horseshoe-shaped mahogany table capable of seating eleven. It was the only piece of furniture he had brought from Earth. The Chief of Security sat on Bertrand's left, across from Dmitri.

I ignored the Knyaz as I sat, turning instead to my left, acknowledging the Caption of Station 1. Across from him sat Duke Stuart Anscomb, a long-time associate of Bertrand.

"General Urakurtz," said Bertrand.

"Ex-general," sniped Dmitri.

I glanced at Dmitri. His nano-enhanced features were more Caucasian than Eurasian. Defiance and malice glinted within his bionic eyes, as did hatred for all things flesh and blood. A visceral need awoke deep within me. I couldn't explain it, but I wanted to crush him. Instead, I ignored the little shit.

So did Bertrand. "Kwami, we have reviewed the vid. Please report."

"Thank you, Counts Palatine. The final tally was five Fleshies dead, two Mark IIs reduced to scrap. I ejected the bodies and pieces into space." I turned to Dmitri. "The third mech, is that a new model?"

Smarmy by nature, Dmitri responded, "Yes. A Petronovich Mark III."

"Ah. They look a lot better than the Mark IIs," I said, "but they smell the same when they're cut in half by a whiner."

Dmitri jumped out of his chair. "You killed it?"

Anger sharpened my voice. "I *destroyed* it." Turning to Stuart, usually the swing vote among the Royals, I went on, "The Mark III attacked and killed Fleshies."

"Are-eh, that's a proper 'arl that," said Stuart, lapsing into his native scouse.

"Cruel? Unfair? Grow up, guttersnipe," said Dmitri. "The Fleshies are reproducing like viruses. We have to keep them in check."

"Bert, we decided," said Stuart. "Mechs may not take Fleshie lives."

"This is going to bring the Planetary Peacekeepers down on us," I added. "We barely escaped their wrath after imprisoning the Fleshies here."

"The Emigration Act did not imprison Fleshies," said Bertrand.

"No, it enslaved them by not allowing them to leave," said Dmitri. "But tell me, Kwami, why do you suddenly care about Fleshies? Why did you let them go? Are you getting soft?"

It was a fair question and I despised Dmitri for asking it. I pushed it aside. "Counts Palatine, allowing mechs to kill Fleshies will inflame the sensibilities of the Terrans. It will remind the Earthers why they exiled us in the first place."

"We were exiled because you couldn't keep your fucking zipper, or your mouth shut!" stormed Dmitri.

I flung back, "Maybe if you hadn't been such a stingy-ass, that reporter would have killed the story."

"You'd have just let your testosterone overcome what few gray cells you actually have and gotten us into trouble again," huffed Dmitri. "I wasn't going to bankrupt the h+ers to pay for your crude appetites."

I'd taken all the backtalk from Dmitri's sniveling little ass that I could stand. I lunged toward Dmitri. The banging of Bertrand's gavel brought me up short. I hated that damn gavel.

"General Urakurtz!" said Bertrand with a final resounding bang.

I gave a Dmitri a last murderous glare before sitting back and clasping my hands together. With my mouth firmly closed, I took a deep breath and slowly exhaled. My agitation subsided. I directed my attention toward Bertrand. "I apologize, Counts Palatine. I have a message from the Fleshie spokesman. They will not allow mechs to man Justice Lock. They'll not be killed by mechs."

"Now we are considering *demands* from the Fleshies?" said Dmitri.

"I suggest we give serious thought to their concerns," I countered.

"Bert," said Dmitri, "half of the Peacekeeper senior officers are our clients. The other half are saving money for their life-lengthening enhancements. Just like the Emigration Act, they will complain and do nothing."

Bertrand looked at me.

My jaw ached. Explaining to these educated idiots that flesh and blood people wouldn't stand for mechs killing them should not have been this hard. Unclenching my teeth, I tried one more time. "Counts Palatine, Fleshie expertise is still necessary. I suggest you listen to them and bend a little."

Bertrand turned to Stuart. "Stuart, have you anything to add?"

"These rock drillers have very aggressive tendencies. I think we should put something in the water to calm them down a bit. Until that happens, I suggest we listen to Kwami."

Dmitri squirmed in his seat.

"Go ahead, Dmitri," said Bertrand.

Here it comes, I thought. *Dmitri's going to throw a wrench in the works.*

"The solution is simple," said Dmitri. "We convert them all to cyborgs."

Incredulous, I jumped out of my chair. "Are you fucking crazy? You can't turn the entire Fleshie population into cyborgs! You'll turn a riot into a revolt."

"Actually, I can." Dmitri turned to Bertrand. "I have portable sick bays ready. We can start with the drillers, then work our way through the families. In the meantime, as per Stuart's suggestion, put contraceptives in the water to stop reproduction."

Bertrand nodded.

I shook my head from side to side. Unable to shake my utter contempt, I rose to leave.

"We have more to discuss, General Urakurtz," said Bertrand.

"I do not have time for discussions, Counts Palatine. If you are going to insist on this disaster, then I have to prepare my troops."

Back in my Security Detachment office, I compartmentalized my burning anger. Allowing it to rage would serve no useful purpose. However, the internal turmoil refused to be quelled. I dug around in my desk until I found the wi-fi enhancer that expanded the functions of my brain chip.

Not wanting to upload, I had accepted only the minimum implant required to sit on the Royal Council. The enhancer gave me access to the rest. I looped it over my ear and connected to the Central Computer. *Play Beethoven, Piano Sonata No. 14 in C Sharp Minor.* At the first notes of the piano, I leaned back and closed my eyes.

Tension eased. Did I really care about the Fleshies? Not really. Maybe a little, but as a Transhumant, I would live forever, long past any human inconvenience.

No, I feared forced conversion. If Dmitri converted the Fleshies to cyborgs, he would push for the conversion of the rest of us. *I will not live in a tin cage. It's not ... human.*

My brain chip's aural alarm blared, dispelling my tranquility. I sat up abruptly. The drilling tunnels on Fourth Level went dark. *Computer, bring the cameras back online.*

Transmission lines have been cut, the computer replied.

Are there any other sensors available?

Transmission lines have been cut.

I was blind.

I ordered, "Alpha Squad, armor up."

Ten minutes later, we deployed to Fourth Level. Exiting the ramps, we turned toward the tunnel lights leading to the drilling area. One by one, they blinked out. My anxiety level shot up. Flipping down my infrared, anti-flash goggles, I plunged through the darkness. On the outer edges of my goggles red dots danced. Five on each side, corresponding to the members of Alpha Squad.

I didn't look forward to what was before us, but at least we would have the advantage in firepower. The pulses of our SR-2s were nasty, vicious, and turned everything it touched into smoking goo, reeking of cooked entrails and could be reconfigured to stun or fire sonic grenades.

The heaviest weapon available to the drillers would be cutters. Built for slicing through iron and granite, these heavy-duty lasers would decimate Fleshie or mech bodies with ease. As tall as two men, counting the sling that carried it, cutters were bulky, unwieldy, and had to tow their charging units behind them on carts.

Half a klick later, we met up with the Fleshies. Alpha Squad approached carefully, giving a wide berth to the Fleshie cutters' field of fire. The Fleshies didn't give me a chance to speak. They let loose with their lasers. We immediately hit the deck and brought our whiners to bear. Instead of landing in our midst, their pulses passed over our heads. I keyed my throat mic and whispered, "Hold your fire."

I spun around and through the after-images of the laser I saw four mechs simply cease to exist. I couldn't believe it. Dmitri had planned the Fleshie conversion in advance. The Council meeting had been a farce.

I Grinned. Dmitri played in my sandbox now. There would be no gavel to stop me. I welcomed the zone. Crabbing to the tunnel wall, I keyed my mic. "Stay down. Hug the edges and face back. We got mechs coming."

I brought up my whiner and fired. It struck a mech chest center, right through its processor. A glowing hole traced its fall. To my left, a blast from the cutters burned a swath through Dmitri's minions. Barking whiners and the bright flashes of the Fleshie lasers illuminated mechs moving forward. Left side firing. Right side moving. Right side firing. Left side moving. The air filled with high-pitched hum of cutter charging units, the taste of iodized oxygen, and rock dust.

Caught between the two fighting units, Alpha Squad had its nuts in a vise. I rose to a crouch. Despite the danger, I meant to dash forward. A brilliant whitish glow seared after images on my retinas as the mech's whiners took out a cutter charging unit. I keyed my mic. "Forward."

We advanced in a staggered motion, half the squad always firing. Behind me I heard a cutter discharge. It burned an arc in the tunnel ceiling ahead of me. For several long moments my lungs refused to draw air. My pulse throbbed in protest. "Fall back," I finally screamed. "Cave in."

I hurled myself backwards. Not far enough. Rubble fell all around. One piece struck my right shoulder just past my chest armor. I felt a sharp slicing sensation. It burned and then subsided. My left arm flailed against the tunnel wall. I threw my right arm forward to cushion my fall. My face tried to carve a furrow in the floor as I landed. I rolled toward the tunnel wall, seeking protection. Thankfully, I retained my goggles, though at some time, I don't remember when, I lost my helmet.

I turned my head to find out why my arm didn't cushion my fall and, through the blood dripping into my eyes, discovered my right arm had been severed at the shoulder. I stared in disbelief. More debris fell, smashing into my hip and legs. Only my armor saved my chest. Through the dim, dust-filled air, I saw movement. A figure approached. I reached for my rifle.

"That's going to hurt like a bitch."

Dmitri. My skin crawled. I wanted to spit the sudden bitter taste out of my mouth. He squatted before me.

"That really sucks about your arm," he said. "It looks like you might bleed out pretty quick."

I didn't need to hear the truth in his voice, I felt it with every spurt of blood that splashed on the tunnel wall. I saw it in the white gleam of bones that used to be my shoulder joint. Dropping adrenaline levels allowed tingles of pain to make it to my brain. Through my grimace, I smiled.

Resigned, I said, "I guess you won't have to put up with me much longer."

"Now where would be the fun in that?" Dmitri asked.

I raised an eyebrow. He tucked his baton-like rod under one arm. With his other he passed a small device over his left leg. A panel opened, and Dmitri removed what appeared to be a square of cloth. He placed it over my shoulder joint. Immediately, the burning ache of severed nerve endings lessened. Arteries knit closed. My eyes widened in surprise.

"Nanos are amazing things, Kwami. As I speak, they are multiplying at phenomenal speed, blocking nerve endings, closing arteries and capillaries, and encouraging re-growth of epidermis cells. They are healing you."

There must have been an opioid infusion in the cloth as well. A sense of euphoria crept up on me. Through the murk, I saw mechs creeping toward the Fleshies and I didn't care. "Why are you helping me?"

"You know, Kwami, we're not so different you and me. Besides, it would be boring here without you and I'm going to need your help on the council."

I laughed. Opiates make everything funny, even helping Dmitri.

Dmitri leaned close and whispered, "You'll have to upload, of course."

There it was, the kicker. Dmitri would save my life *if* I became a mech like him. I laughed again.

"Look at this body, Kwami."

Dmitri raised my leg out of the rubble. If I wasn't watching him, I wouldn't have known it. He wrapped his mechanical fingers around my ankle and squeezed. The bones snapped as they crushed.

Stabbing needles of agony broke through the opioid haze. I may have screamed. I don't remember.

"This body is so fragile," Dmitri continued. "It's completely ruined. What do you say, Kwami? This is your last chance. Upload and be made whole."

I hefted my whiner up before my face. With my thumb hidden from Dmitri's view, I keyed my throat mic and left it open. "I'd have to stand ready."

"Ready for what?" asked Dmitri.

In my goggles I saw six dots light up. Within me a warm glow competed with the relaxing effects of the numbing drug. Alpha Squad had survived the cave-in. I commanded, "Fire."

Six whiners screamed in the dark. They laid down a continuous field of fire. Four took out mechs ahead of me. Two struck Dmitri. The pulses came in level with his waist then bent up as they neared the Knyaz, striking him in the head.

Through the infrared lens of my goggles, Dmitri's head glowed. The high-pitched whine devolved into a low-pitched growl, then ceased. Amazingly, Dmitri rose, unscathed, to his full height.

I stared open mouthed. Never had I seen anything like it.

Dmitri smiled and pointed to a braided, coppery wire he wore around his forehead and temples like a circlet. "What do you think? I call it a Halo.

Ingenious, isn't it? It's like an energy wave magnet, drawing and absorbing all beam weapons."

He raised his baton and pointed it down tunnel. Two beams shot out from it. Two of my men screamed. "It also returns the energy to its source. It's an ELF. Extreme Low Frequency. I'm really quite fond of it."

In my drug-induced state, I could think of nothing to say. The echo of pounding footsteps drifted to us from up tunnel. Fleshies swarmed out of the darkness. They filled the tunnel with beams from lasers and a few whiners. Dmitri's mechs, already depleted by battle and the cave in, took heavy casualties. They fell back.

Dmitri studied the onrushing Fleshies. "Hmm, I may have to revise my opinion of Fleshies." Dmitri cut his gaze back to me. "Goodbye, Kwami. Enjoy your last few moments with your new friends." He pointed his baton at me.

I stared stupidly at it.

Several shots from hand lasers and whiners slammed into Dmitri's Halo. He quivered as if he suffered a systems overload. His baton loosed a long blast of crackling energy. Instead of striking me, the beam sped off in the direction of the lasers that struck the Halo. The baton's energy spent, Dmitri turned and scrambled over the fallen rock debris, going back the way he came. He disappeared in the murk.

I released the breath I didn't know I held. I was safe. Four red dots remained on the side of my goggles. I tried to get comfortable. My shoulder and leg injuries had quit bleeding, but broken bones prevented any position of comfort.

Out of the gloom materialized the Fleshie spokesman from the Holding Cells. He stopped in front of me.

"It *is* you. You saved us. We thought the cave-in got them all. We'd already left. Your firing brought us back. If not for you, they'd have ambushed us." He put his finger to his ear bud and nodded. A smile spread slowly across his face. He said, "Instead, we're driving them back all the way to the plaza."

I should have felt gratitude, but numbness overrode my feelings. "Do you know who I am?"

The spokesman took out his knife and cut his palm. He held up his bleeding hand. "I know you, Kwami Urakurtz. I know this, too. You bleed."

He pointed to two men. "Dig him out. The rest of you, gather up the dropped weapons."

Suddenly tired, I rested my head against the tunnel wall. I needed to sleep.

The tunnel rumbled. I looked up. A single chunk of granite dislodged and fell from the ceiling. My world went dark.

I opened my eyes. A sense of oddness blunted my awareness. I could see, but it was different. Sharper. Clearer. I looked around. I was in a small sickbay, lying in a sani-bed. *What happened? How did I get here?*

Sitting up, I heard the tiniest sound of a servo. I caught a sense of motion and looked toward the door. Through it walked the Fleshie spokesman. With him was a smaller man in a white lab coat.

"I'm Doctor Wood. How do you feel? Does everything work?" asked the man in the coat.

"Work?" I brought my right hand up and scratched my forehead. I pulled it down before my eyes and gasped, "My right hand." My breath came haltingly. "But ... but." I looked around, unable to focus on any one thing. Memories of the fight in the tunnel, the cave in, and Dmitri spun rapidly around my new reality. I didn't know which to believe. "But, I lost my arm."

"Along with both legs," said the spokesman.

I heard his words but could not comprehend their meaning.

"It was the nanos that kept you alive," said the doctor.

It all came back to me. The oddness I experienced upon waking returned. Something cold and impersonal took over my awareness. I remembered a chunk of granite falling from the ceiling and smashing into my face. My subconscious had suppressed the memory. Now something else controlled memory function. Something detached, unemotional.

I touched my head. "How much?"

"Brain loss? Eighty percent." The doctor hurried on, "I saved as much as I could. Fortunately, the Knyaz left this portable sickbay behind when he ran away. Well stocked, too. It had the latest in AIs. With you being who you are, I took the opportunity to implant the same Wi-Fi interfaces shared by the rest of the Royal Council."

No. No. No. Devastated, I lay back down and whispered, "Thank you."

I didn't see them leave. Despite my new AI, self-pity washed over me like a huge wave. Dmitri did this to me. *He will pay.* I tasted the bitter irony that soured my mouth. I had refused to upload, refused to give up my pretty face. Now, my pretty face was gone. Neither human nor mech, but the worst of both worlds, I was a cyborg.

I cried.

My Crazy Uncle Ba'al

Ba'al shivered as he closed his office door on the bitter cold of the Gleven See winter. Scientists had recently declared the planet in the Goldilocks zone. Ba'al harrumphed. "If that's the case, this Goldilocks must be one of the hair-covered Gleven."

Gleven See's chief historian shuffled to his desk and flopped into his chair. The weight of his concerns robbed him of more and more of his strength every day. He had to find a successor.

KNOCK, KNOCK, KNOCK.

Ba'al looked up. "Is Darius here already? Is he early? Am I late?"

He poured himself a glass of water and reached into his desk drawer for one of the pills his doctor pushed on him. It was for his heart, or circulation, or some such nonsense.

"Come in."

Darius entered. Barely a season past his age of responsibility, he still looked an adolescent. Not even his short beard or moustache added age. Only the trimming of his mane, the hand-width band of hair running from the back of his neck to waist, marked his adulthood. He stopped a pace inside the door.

Ba'al swallowed his pill and picked up his stylus. He tapped it against his chin, studying his nephew. "Well, come closer. I don't bite. Despite the stories."

The young man shifted from foot to foot. He surveyed the office. If the ceiling-to-floor bookcases filled with scrolls and books with rudimentary bindings impressed him, he gave no indication.

Ba'al withheld judgment, for the moment at least. "So, you're Darius."

Darius stared back firmly. "And you're crazy Uncle Ba'al."

Ba'al chuckled. "Spoken like my sister's son. I've often accused her of having some Coven in her. Come, sit down." Ba'al used his stylus to indicate the chair before his desk. "Are you here out your own interest or did she make you show up?"

Darius took off his long cloak. Made from the thrice combed and twirled hair of the Aruk, tightly weft and shaved before beaten into a supple softness, it provided the main source of income for the women of his mother's clan. He hung it on the peg beside the door.

Like his uncle, he wore long trousers and a collarless, long sleeve shirt. He also had a pair of darkened glasses tucked in his neckline. "For some reason my mother believes this is a good idea. Mogg only knows why. Your name causes her a lot of grief in the community."

"My name?" asked Ba'al. "Or is it your association with the newest manifestation of spiritual enlightenment?"

Darius did a double take. "You know?"

Ba'al sat straighter. He'd heard the stories of the half-breed Coven, part Gleven, part Mel Chor, spewing his version of the past across the major towns of Gleven See, disguising his distortions as religion. And he knew of the young Leven that often stood at his side. Ba'al's mane quivered under his shirt. "I'll tell you what I know. The Leven did not swing out of trees one day and suddenly decide to be human."

Darius took a seat in the chair before Ba'al's desk. The change in subject affected Darius immediately. His eyes brightened. His voice took on the tone of wonderment. "No, we did not. Mogg experienced a visit on a summer day. The creator, who cannot be named, told him of a great transformation. A change that would alter the Gleven forever—"

"Let me guess," said Ba'al. "Children of the chosen will grow to be taller and more intelligent. Human speech will be taught to them. They will learn how to till the soil and tame the wild beasts. They will lose the hair that covers most of their bodies—"

"Yes!" said Darius, excited.

Ba'al shook his head.

The great Lady had warned him. Remnants of the Melchoirian genetical experiments survived on Gleven See. They roamed the countryside distorting ancient history, stirring up the populace, preparing the Leven for a Melchoirian return. "An interesting story. Where this Mogg goes wrong is in the origination and its conclusion."

Darius leaned back in his chair and folded his arms across his chest.

"The first time I heard it," continued Ba'al, ignoring his nephew's response, "my grandfather Rueben, your great-great uncle, told it. The second time, I heard it in more detail from the creator herself."

Darius gasped. His eyes widened, and then narrowed in anger. "You mock me."

Ba'al wet his lips. He needed Darius, but his sister's son must accept the truth. With a slow deliberate movement, he set his stylus down and squared himself to face Darius directly. "The creator's name is Lieutenant S'rah, from the planet Celeste. She is a medical officer of the Fleet of the Most High—"

"Blasphemy!"

The outburst caused a fluttering in his chest. He set his jaw and breathed in slowly. "She is the one that changed us. She took the Gleven, the original inhabitants of our planet and altered them. We, the Leven, are the result."

Darius' face reddened. His fists tightened, whitening his knuckles. "I don't know why Mother believes in you. However, I can tell you this; the followers of Mogg do not. We were uplifted by Melchoirians."

Ba'al shook his head.

Darius' anger propelled him forward. "Yes! And if you must know, Mother did send me here to listen to what you have to offer, but if its ridicule and conspiracy theories, then I'll have none of it!"

Ba'al jumped up. He pounded his fist on his desk. "First words! The truth. Not theory."

Darius shook. Through clenched teeth, he said, "No, Uncle, you are wrong. And you can find some other fool for whatever it is you want."

Ba'al sat down hard. His heart pounded. *Relax. Breathe slowly.* He closed his eyes. When he opened them again, he saw Darius at the door putting on his cloak. Ba'al needed Darius. He needed him to stay. He tried an appeal to his nephew's studious nature. "Do you read imprint?"

Darius paused. Few now remembered Leven's earliest form of writing. He studied Ba'al through hooded lids. "Yes."

Ba'al spoke softly, "I can prove my words. I have tablets."

Darius' gaze lingered for a moment longer. Her resumed putting on his cloak. "I don't believe you."

Ba'al had no strength to defend his claim. His heart continued to pound erratically. He leaned his head back against the wall and closed his eyes. The door opened and shut. Ba'al rummaged around in his drawer for another pill.

"Damn! Why did I have to attack?"

Ba'al wouldn't admit it, especially to himself, but he was afraid. He feared he did not have enough time left to find someone to take up his mission. As much as he railed against his doctor, Ba'al could not deny the increasing failure of his heart. He had dismissed it for some time. As a result, he put off finding an apprentice. Now the arrhythmic episodes occurred daily. He had no choice but to depend on Darius.

"If he comes back, I'll be nicer. I'll be persuasive."

Ba'al took several deep breaths. His heart rate stabilized. He decided to go to his sister's house. He would go to Darius to show him his sincerity. It would be a token of penance. Decision made, Ba'al rose to his feet.

The door opened. Darius walked in. Ba'al's breath caught in his throat. "Darius, I ... I was on my way to your mother's. I'm sorry. I spoke harshly."

Darius fumbled for words. "Yes, well, I'm sorry, too. You're family. I should at least give you the benefit of doubt." Interest sparkled in his eyes. "Do you really have tablets of Imprint?"

Ba'al smiled inwardly. "So that's what brought you back. Inquisitiveness runs in the family."

"Some would say it is our curse," said Darius.

"Indeed," said Ba'al. "Have a seat. Get comfortable."

While Darius shed his cloak, Ba'al went to a special cabinet, one of the few devices left behind by the Celestials. Within the climate-controlled interior, Ba'al stored soft clay tablets. He selected one and returned to his desk. Darius waited, once again sitting in the chair before the desk. Picking up his stylus, Ba'al swiftly marked the tablet. He slid it to Darius.

His nephew cocked his head and raised an eyebrow. "You write Imprint?"

"Yes. Lt. S'rah taught me. I wrote a good portion of the tablets still in existence. My grandfather wrote a large portion of the rest. Many have been lost or destroyed."

Darius looked as if his uncle had betrayed his good will. He seemed ready to bolt. "I thought the tablets would be historical."

Ba'al checked his anger. He reminded himself that he needed Darius and he needed him to believe. "Read this one first. Then if you are still interested, I'll get you a *historical* one."

Darius didn't back down or apologize for the slight. He spun the tablet around and read, "I swear that what I say is the truth, the whole truth, and nothing but the truth." Darius' cheeks colored slightly. He asked, "What is this last symbol?"

"My scribe's mark," said Ba'al. "We all had one. Official tablets required the mark of the scribe who wrote it."

"None of Mogg's tablets have a mark."

"Then they are not official. Mogg is not on the list."

Darius' head popped up. "What list? How do you know that?"

"The List of Scribes. I have it in the other room,"

"Mogg's a Scaly, at least part. That probably explains it."

Ba'al trod lightly. He could ill-afford to offend his nephew. "By Scaly, you mean Coven."

Darius crossed his arms over his chest once again. His haughty attitude returned, "So now you are going to get all racist on me. 'We can't trust him because he is different than us.'"

Ba'al fought back the urge to defend the truth vigorously. He needed to sound reasonable, not 'crazy.' "No, that is not what I'm saying at all. I've read his Better Way. It is a prelude to acceptance of a Melchoirian invasion."

"No! It is a promise. It will enrich our lives."

"It is an empty vessel. He has no way to deliver. The Melchoirians lost the war. After that, Lt. S'rah made me a promise."

Darius rose to his feet. He looked down on his uncle. "And what *promise* did this S'rah make? Salvation? World peace?"

Ba'al stilled his face, but he couldn't still his sinking disappointment. He'd made a mistake counting on Darius, but that mistake couldn't kill his pride. "She promised to make us Star People."

Darius' eyebrows knit together until they almost touched. He seemed confused. "She promised what?"

"To continue to give us the knowledge we need to eventually be like the Celestials. To eventually travel to other stars. Other planets."

Darius slowly closed his mouth. He sat down, stunned. "By Mogg, the stories are true. You're a cracked nut."

Ba'al took a deep breath. His nephew's words hurt, a lot, but he couldn't give up. "You wanted a historical tablet. Wait here. I'll be right back."

Darius nodded, but it wasn't very convincing.

Ba'al went to the door of his adjoining room. He gave his nephew a last glance before unlocking the door. Darius tapped his darkened glasses in the palm of his hand, looking bored. Ba'al disappeared into the room, returning a moment later with two clay tablets. He carefully placed them on his desk in front of Darius.

"Start with this one."

Darius' eyes hungrily took in the ancient tablet. He lightly ran his fingers over the cuneiform script. He lifted his gaze to his uncle. "You wrote this?"

Ba'al picked up his old stylus and tapped it against his chin. "Yes, I did."

It is old," said Darius.

"And so am I," harrumphed Ba'al. "One day you, too, will be old. If you are lucky. Read."

Darius read. When finished, he pushed away the first clay tablet. He sat back and stroked his upper lip and chin, smoothing down his close-cropped beard and mustache."

The accounts of the clash between the Celestials and Melchiorians had not generated the interest Ba'al hoped. He sensed a hardening of his nephew's resolve. *He doesn't believe.*

Darius blinked one time, slowly. His unflinching gaze bore into Ba'al. "You mean to say that the Better Way is not just a promise? That there already *is* life on other planets and that they are more advanced than we are?"

"Yes, that is what I say."

Darius closed his eyes and shook his head.

Ba'al continued, "Since you are so enamored of the Coven, read the second tablet. You might find it interesting."

Interesting might not have been the right word. As Darius read, his neck muscles tensed and corded. The vein from his temple to his forehead throbbed. He violently pushed the tablet away from him and leaped up. "Blasphemy!"

Ba'al lurched forward, afraid his nephew would destroy the rare tablets. A sharp pain stabbed pain his chest, the same reoccurring pain that had prompted

Ba'al to send for his nephew in the first place. Only this time Ba'al's heart pounded hard once, twice, then a third time. Each beat felt like a blow from a Coven, hammering on his chest. Ba'al fell back in his chair. Short, choppy gasps did not allow any air into his lungs. Beads of sweat formed on his forehead, coming together to trickle down into his eyes.

Concern replaced the religious fervor that had dominated Darius' face. "Uncle?"

Ba'al's eyes lost focus. Time slowed. Finally, with a gasping start, his heart beat again, its rhythm irregular. Fast, like the rapid tattoo of a drum in triplets. Then slow. His lungs drew in large breaths. He felt a cloth mopping the sweat from his brow. His heartbeat normalized. Vision returning, Ba'al brushed his nephew's hands away.

"I'm fine. I'm fine."

"Are you sure?" asked Darius. "You look pale."

Ba'al wasn't fine and he knew it. He hovered on the cusp of another attack. He no longer had the luxury of time to convince his nephew to carry on in his stead. He needed an answer now. There remained one last proof. "If you want the truth, pick up the tablets and follow me."

A more subdued Darius, carefully cradling the clay tablets, followed Ba'al into the adjoining room. Upon entering, lights in the ceiling turned on. Sturdy shelves containing row after row of clay tablets and crudely bound books lined the walls of the small library. Ba'al heard the sudden intake of breath behind him. "Do not drop the tablets." He leaned against the one table in the center of the room. "Place them here. Follow me."

A door in the far-right corner provided the only other exit. Ba'al shuffled over to the door and waited for Darius to join him. Once again, opening the door triggered the lighting, bathing the stairwell in brightness. A life-sized portrait of a woman with straight red hair and, other than her elongated skull, smooth, hairless skin greeted them. The slight tilt to her eyes gave her an intriguing and, in Ba'al's opinion, compassionate look. She wore a single piece jumpsuit and held some sort of device in her hand.

"She has no mane," said Darius. "Who is that?"

The awe in Darius' voice warmed Ba'al's soul. "More blasphemy. Her name is S'rah. Come along."

His nephew followed silently. The stairs went halfway up the wall before reversing and ending up above the library. Ba'al rested on the first landing. Sweat beaded his forehead.

"Uncle, is this necessary?" asked Darius. "You are weak. Maybe we should wait until you are better."

Ba'al knew there would be no getting better. He lurched onward. "I'm as good as I'm going to be. Come along."

The door at the top of the stairs opened into a room slightly larger than a closet. A contoured chair, surrounded by panels on three sides, dominated the room. Ba'al leaned on the doorjamb, his chest heaving.

Gritting his teeth, he said, "Take me to the chair."

Darius supported his uncle as best he could as they made their way the few steps and into the chair.

The chair molded to the curves of Ba'al's body, cradling it. Ba'al sighed in relief and closed his eyes. His heartbeat calmed. He had forgotten how well the chair induced relaxation. He motioned with his hand for his nephew to sit at his feet.

He heard the rustle of clothes and picked up on Darius' soft oohs. Ba'al opened one eye to see his nephew reach tentatively to touch the chair.

"Uncle, what is it?"

"A transportation and communications console. It is a gift from the Teachers. The most important thing they left behind. Now hush and listen. You've already read the transcript telling you who is speaking. So, for now, listen."

Ba'al touched a button on the chair's armrest. Voices emanated from speakers embedded in the chair. A klaxon blared.

" Aaroo-aa-aaroo-aa-aaroo-aa. General Quarters. General Quarters. All personnel man your battle stations."

Darius jumped back, looking rapidly left and right. He started to speak. Ba'al hushed him with a hand motion.

"Captain to the bridge. Captain to the bridge."

"Status!"

"Sir, we were hailing Lieutenant S'rah. The planet responded with sonic pulses."

Darius interrupted. "The woman in the painting?"

Ba'al smiled. He had expected accusations of blasphemy. "Yes, Darius. Now remain silent."

"Any response from Lieutenant S'rah?"

"None, sir. I've hailed on all frequencies."

"Captain, there's a shuttle rising off the planet. Now there are two, make that three, shuttles. They are heading for the dark side of the planet. Sir, the last one is the Captain's Barge."

"Launch a probe. I want to know what is hiding back there. Comm, have the Bila widen out in the direction those shuttles are taking."

"Aye, sir."

"Message sent, Captain."

"I want that barge. I want to know why they fired. Launch four interceptors. Two on CAP, two shooters. Have four more on standby."

"Comm, hail the barge. Have you found any sign of Lieutenant S'rah?"

"No, sir."

"Very well, keep looking."

"Captain, I have the barge."

"On screen."

"Captain Elo, what a surprise."

"Luc. So, you escaped and ran off to the Sultan of Mel Chor."

At the gasp from Darius, Ba'al paused the recording. He hadn't wanted to. He had been reliving the day in the Red Mountains when he had first heard it. It was the same day he had watched the Coven fight. He opened his eyes. "Yes, Darius."

"Uncle Ba'al, are they ... flying?"

"Yes, Darius. They are. Isn't it glorious?"

"But," Darius struggled for words, "how is it possible?"

Ba'al heart fluttered, reminding him of his limited time. "They are the Teachers, Darius. The true teachers. You must follow them."

"But, Uncle, I have promised Mogg."

Ba'al's breath came in shallower measures. "You must break your promise to him. Promise to me. Where do think the knowledge of the Leven comes from? This room."

"That cannot be."

Ba'al convulsed. His chest rose from the contours of the chair before settling back down. A new voice beckoned from the speakers.

"Ba'al? This is Admiral S'rah. Do you read me?"

Ba'al barely managed a blissful whisper. "Great Lady, you have come."

"I gave my word, Counselor Ba'al. My sensors indicate another presence. Is this your replacement?"

Ba'al raised an inquiring eyebrow at Darius. He'd wagered everything on this moment. "Well, nephew?"

Darius looked shocked. His eyes opened wide, his mouth hung open. He moved his lips, but no sound came out.

Ba'al could offer no more encouragement. He'd spent his last reserves.

Finally, Darius nodded.

Ba'al slumped back in the chair and closed his eyes. His breath slowly exhaled. Weakly, between gasps, Ba'al said, "It is, Great Lady. He is Darius. He will be Leven's representative. But he is young."

"We all were once, Ba'al. Well done," said S'rah with warmth. "Prepare yourself to come aboard. S'rah out."

Ba'al thought she sounded pleased.

Darius spluttered, "You're leaving?"

"Yes, nephew. My part is done. It is now up to you to fulfill the completion of the Great Lady's promise. Under your leadership the Leven will become Star People."

"What have I done? I can't do this. Uncle, you must stay. You must help me."

Ba'al felt himself fading. He turned his head toward Darius and smiled. "You'll do fine."

THE DAWNING BLOSSOMED into a fine day. The crisp air, calm wind, and brightly shining sun put a spring in Darius' step. A faint siren sounded. Darius turned. In the distance, a bright yellow glow appeared underneath the tall rocket. Accompanied by the roar and smoke of Celestial-assisted Leven technology, it rose slowly and majestically into the sky.

Darius turned away, his face a picture of satisfaction and fulfillment. He entered the stairwell that would take him down to a small room. In this room was a chair, the chair that would take him home. Too old and frail to use a rocket to rendezvous with Minister Adam, Darius would instead use the transporter. The same one that had taken his Uncle Ba'al a life time ago. He wondered if uncle would greet him.

Darius made himself comfortable in the chair. The air cocooned around him, swirling. A soothing hum filled his ears. At the other end of this journey lay the fulfilling of a promise. The Most High Federation of Planets would grow by one. The Leven would be Star People. His little closet disappeared.

The Road to Damascus

The winking red light on my comm unit refused to be ignored. Only a select few had access to the very secure, very private channel and I knew who waited on the other end. Suppressing the indicator, I muttered under my breath, "Not now, I'm busy."

"What was that, Captain?" asked the helm officer.

"Get me the Captains."

"Aye, sir."

Four holograms pixilated before me. Anshar, Elish, Apsu, and finally, the Second for this mission, Marduk.

"We have a tight schedule on this one," I began with a pointed look at Marduk. "No time for grandstanding. Drop in, pick up the cargo, and get out. Understood?"

My glare continued to rest on Marduk.

Marduk sat silent, not bothering to hide his scowl.

"Any questions?"

"Tell me, Sargon, what good is it being a God if you don't get to do godly things?" groused Marduk.

I nipped it in the bud. "At Orpheus 2, you command. On Siris 7, I command. You can wait to be a God until then. Or you can feel free to contact the Igigi and take up your godly ambitions with them." I paused for the briefest of moments before continuing. "Elish, move the ships into position."

I didn't wait for an acknowledgement. I cut the channel and slammed back into my chair. "Huh. I'm going to have to do something about Marduk before Marduk does something about me."

Siris 7, the dazzling blue planet on the forward display, was as good a place as any to resolve the issue. The winking red light on my comm unit returned. *Give it a break*. I rose. "I'll be in my cabin."

"Aye, Captain."

I knew what awaited me. Bathaal, the Messiah-prophet placed on Siris 7 to guide the populace into submission. Recently, he had developed a conscious. I retired to my cabin to see what my clone had to say.

The hologram sharpened into focus. It still jolted me to see the same arrogant stance, the same straight black hair, the same slanted eyes staring back at me. The difference between us being, I would not revolt against orders. That realization sharpened the edge of my frustration. "Yes, what is it?"

"Father, you are angry with me," said the soft-spoken Messiah-prophet.

I winced. Several times over the last century, I had tried to get my clone to stop addressing me as Father. It had proven wasted breath. "I don't have time for this. What is your purpose?"

"To be the gateway and the light. To bring the souls of my brethren to a better place by your side—"

I immediately regretted my phrasing, "So what's the problem?"

"These new teachings of my successor, Father Franklin, are they true? Am I, are you, no more than an alien?"

At the edge of the clone's words, I heard a something. *Anger? Betrayal?* I didn't want to get drawn into a philosophical discussion, I asked brusquely, "Does it matter?"

"I am tasked to bring these people to their salvation. But if you are not their god, then it would be bondage. Would *you* be a slave?"

A jolt of fury tore through me. The question hit too close to recent thoughts of my own. I snarled, "What do you know about it? You know nothing about wearing a yoke!"

"I know how you feel about the Igigi."

How could you possibly know? You have never lived under the thumb of the Igigi! Railing at my irritating clone would serve no purpose. I got a grip on my emotions and, terminating the connection, headed back to the bridge. Trouble would come of this. I knew it.

One day a week all the peoples of the planet gathered in their town squares. The large prominent viewscreens allowed everyone to see and hear Father Franklin, the recently appointed head of the Sirisian religious community, deliver his sermon. The Good News, he called it. I had not missed one of the closely monitored sermons since my arrival.

Entering the bridge, I said, "It is time for the Good News. On screen."

Father Franklin raised his hands in supplication. "Salvation is near, though none knoweth the hour."

Playing to the bridge crew, I interjected, "I do. That's why we're here."

They chuckled.

Father Franklin continued, "In our Father's house are many mansions. He has prepared a place for you. He will come again and receive you into his bosom."

I said to myself, "If you only knew."

The Igigi, the master race, survived on the life-force of other races. The harvest of life-energy from Siris 7 would secure my position in the Igigi hierarchy for a long time. If Marduk or even the clone thought they could alter this harvest, I would deal with them swiftly, and harshly.

In synchronized precision, the five-ship armada, orbiting just above the exosphere, completed their repositioning. One real ship and four holographic images orbited above each landing site. I had no fear of planet-side defenses. My agents had long since infiltrated the government, military, and all socio-religious aspects of the planet's culture. I owned the planet lock, stock, and barrel. The Sirisians existed solely to be a food source. The ships reported directly above the assigned landing zones.

"Marduk, status."

"All ships on station and ready."

"Initiate salvation sequence. Execute on my command."

"Aye, sir," replied Marduk.

Projection arrays slid out on narrow rails, rotated, and locked on assigned targets. Launchers, loaded with pods filled with electronic transmitters and image enhancers, homed in to specific areas of the troposphere below, areas that, for the last decade, had been saturated with chem trails. Barium sulfate, aluminum, and desiccated red blood cells not only enhanced the electronic signals, but, over time, help render the populace submissive.

I typed a string of codes into my comm then sat back, waiting as slower, less sophisticated computers of the local inhabitants went through their security protocols. The spinning icon stopped. My image replaced that of Father Franklin on the huge screens below. "Father Franklin."

The Sirisian priest broke off imploring the swift arrival of the planet's Savior. "Lord!"

In the background, the enthusiastic voices of the masses attending the event hushed in silent awe. I did not bother to hide or diffuse my pleasure at being worshipped; besides, I did intend to save them. I would save them from the monotony of mere existence by allowing them to sacrifice their life-energy for the greater good. Mine. "Father Franklin, all is in readiness?"

"Yes, Lord Sargon."

"Well done, Father Franklin." I tapped another code into my armrest controls. "Marduk, what is the status of the 'salvation' sequence."

"All systems up and running. Systems check complete. No anomalies."

I made one last check of my screens. Not that I didn't trust Marduk, but because I didn't trust Marduk.

"Execute." The real ships slowly descended, heading for their assigned landing sites. I turned my attention planet side. "Father Franklin, I believe you have an announcement to make."

Father Franklin's trembling visage replaced mine on the screens. With simplicity and sincerity, Father Franklin spoke into the microphone.

"Friends, fellow faithful,"

I knew that not all planet-side believed. Some always hung back, distrusting the forward strides of their religious leaders, discounting the technological advances, disavowing the new doctrines so carefully and strategically introduced, especially the newest one.

The Messiah is a child from space.

"The truth of the Good News is upon us!" intoned Father Franklin.

The throats of thousands roared their approval. Above each landing zone, my image materialized in the cerulean sky. Gazing down benignly and lovingly, the image spread its arms wide in welcome. Around it ships appeared, hovering over the gathering.

"Behold! The Messiah! He has come! Come for his children. Come to gather all to his bosom. Let none be afraid," proclaimed Father Franklin.

At each site, a single ship descended. At my LZ, the capitol city, the old cleric gathered his closest advisors, formed a processional, and made his way through the crowd. His ecstatic voice commanded, "Make your way to the welcoming. Orderly! Remain orderly!"

The loading proceeded smoothly. The deluded masses willingly climbed the ramps. I, or a holographic image of me, met them at the top of the ramp and offered encouragement as they disappeared into the bowels of the huge space-going ships. Their Savior had come to take them to the promised land.

After personally greeting the first two or three thousand, I stepped aside. Protocol satisfied, I hurried to the bridge. The blistering voice of Marduk provided the cadence for my footsteps.

"It's that crazy clone of yours. He's advancing on the southern landing and he has a small army with him."

I shed the robe I had worn as the Messiah and tapped a sequence of buttons on the wrist-comm of my Nephilim ship suit. The heads-up display activated, giving me real-time readouts from the tac-comm. "What the—"

My clone did have a small army. "Those weapons are of Nephilim design."

"This is your doing," said Marduk. "The Igigi will hear of this."

"Throw a contain field around him and move the holo-ships in your zone towards him. That should hold him off."

"I'll take care of your clone. Then I'll take care of you, traitor."

Entering the bridge, I imagined dissecting Marduk, cutting out all the treasonous parts, and throwing what little remained to the Igigi. None on the bridge spoke as I sat in the Captain's chair and opened the storage compartment under the armrest on my right side. I extracted the Corona, so called because of the yellowish glow it emitted when worn. With it on and activated, I could fully integrate all the ship's computers and control them with a mere thought. The seldom-used Corona meant one thing, battle.

But who am I going to fight? I slipped it on, wincing as the probes anchored themselves to my skull, and receptors plunged ultra-thin needles into my brain. The information from the sensors of all five ships appeared before me.

I could see the contain field Marduk had put around the advancing Sirisians. It held for the moment but continued to weaken under the concentrated assault of the attackers. *Damn that clone!* I opened a channel to him and snapped, "What do think you are doing? Cease fire this instant!"

"Why should we? You have betrayed us!" shouted the clone.

"Bathaal, don't do this."

"Father. You have called me by my name. You have not done this thing in a long time," said the clone, the angry edge of his voice blunted. "Why now?"

Surprise flashed through me. And annoyance. I had not meant to address the clone as anything other than that. Clone. I cursed myself. *Fool!* "Look," I began harshly, "if you break through the contain field you and your followers will die."

"Better one death as a free man than a thousand as a slave," said the clone. "Wouldn't you agree?"

"What do you know of slavery?"

"I know that you are one," said the clone. "I feel the Igigi chains around your ankles. I see the Igigi yoke across your shoulders and its well-worn groove. I know that it chafes you."

The clone's piercing perception cut to my soul. I could not deny his words. For decades I continually told myself that I had to integrate myself in the Igigi's good graces before I could act. Was I lying to myself? With a pain-filled voice, I said, "It is true my Nephilim heritage screams for release, but now is not the time."

"There is never a good time," said the clone. "Prepare to learn."

What's he talking about? I scanned the sensors. Other than the weakening of the contain field, I saw no abnormalities. "Learn what?"

"Watch."

The screens before my eyes blanked. Irritated, I demanded, "What are you doing to my screens?"

"Your screens are now blank, save one."

One of the screens came back to life.

"What do you see?"

I steeled myself against the scene. "Sirisians are dying as the Igigi feed. What has this to do with me?"

"You play God, Father. It may surprise you to know that there is one. And he is displeased."

My irritation morphed with the display on the screen. Horror replaced it. "The images ... it is no longer Sirisians dying. It is Nephilim."

"That is what will happen, Father. God has decreed it. Unless ... you put an end to this abomination."

I refused to believe what my eyes witnessed. As long as I provided the Igigi with souls, they'd promised to leave the Nephilim alone. "That's impossible. You're hacking the computer. You're generating these images."

"No, Father. It is very possible. Perhaps you are not persuaded."

To my horror, the familiar hum of the ship's operation faded to an eerie silence. The hair on my arms and at the back of my neck stood on end. I shivered. The spell lasted but a moment. Frantic calls from the helmsman a few feet away from me broke the trance.

"Captain, we've lost all power."

"The cargo?"

"Three quarters loaded."

I tried to reach out to the other ships and realized that despite the Corona, I had no sense of them. Icy fingers of panic gripped me. I fought back. "What's happening? What did you do?"

"I did nothing," said the helmsman.

"It is the work of God," said the clone.

My thoughts raced back to my youth and the teachings of Nephilim divinity. I couldn't grasp them. Time and again, my thoughts diverted back to the images of the Igigi feeding off my people. *Is it true? Is there a greater God?* I had no answer. "What would you have me do?"

The question met with silence. I reached out again to ask my clone, but the connection had been severed. The chains of the Igigi weighed heavy around my ankles. The background hum of ship's power returned.

"Captain, power is returning. Normal operations are restored. What just happened?"

I ignored the Helmsman's question. Via the Corona, I ran a complete scan of operational systems, checking for any evidence of outside intrusions. I found nothing. "Summoned the captains."

They responded quickly. All, that is, but Marduk, whose screen remained blank. *How unsurprising.* I moved straight to the point. "The clone has mounted an armed resistance in Marduk's sector. Marduk is doing what he can to minimize the damage. Discontinue loading. Be ready to depart immediately."

I replaced the screens of the captains with tactical screens giving battlefield assessments. The contain field held for the moment but could breach at any time. If—no, when—the clone's followers broke free, they would ignore the holo-ships and head directly for the only real ship in the sector. Of that I had no doubt. I did not believe they could damage it, but they should not have been able to shoot their way out of a contain field either.

My Igigi superiors will not be pleased with me coming in under quota. My quirky smile was fleeting. *One thing at a time,* I reminded myself. *First, minimize Marduk.*

My second stood out like a sore thumb. Thirty klicks in front of Bathaal's forces, Marduk had climbed atop the gateway of a park entrance. He undoubtedly planned to do something 'Godly' like taking out my clone and his followers. That would send a message to the Igigi.

I also knew a little about sending messages. I set up a secure path with the Corona and programmed my instructions into Marduk's ship.

Over the planet-side viewscreens, a stern, computer-generated image of myself replaced the pre-recorded boarding instructions of Father Franklin. Under it, I ran a soundtrack of weapons fire and explosions. I pumped up the volume enough to overwhelm the local's senses and awe them into submission.

"How dare you defy me! I am your Creator. Pay the price of disobedience."

The display on the huge screens switched to holo-ships firing down on the crowd. In the Southern section the action was real. Sirisians scattered before my image, looking for cover. The ramp of Marduk's ship retracted and the huge craft lifted slowly skyward.

Marduk spared a look back at his departing ship. His unsuppressed rage contorted his features into a hideous mask.

"You're a coward, Sargon! An embarrassment to the Nephilim. The Igigi will put me in your place."

Though none could see it, I smiled with cold assurance. "I don't think so."

Marduk charged his shoulder-fired grenade launcher.

I detected a shaped charge projectile, one of the few hand-held weapons that could penetrate a contain field.

Ignoring his departing ship, Marduk raised his weapon and sighted.

I fired first.

To Sirisians on the ground it looked as if two beams of light escaped from the contain field. The first took Marduk and disintegrated him. The next burned its way into the bridge of Marduk's ship. The globe shaped vessel stopped rising and descended back to the surface, landing hard. It listed toward the bent stabilizing strut and settled amid a cloud of dust.

In retaliation, a single blaster cannon from Marduk's ship fired twice in rapid succession. The first burst the contain field. The second erupted at the last known position of the clone. The screens and sensors of all five ships blanked.

I checked the scans. The modifications I made to the sensors held. None indicated any sign of my clone or his army. I restored communications and the altered sensors to the remaining ships and opened a channel to the armada. The Captains were talking over each other as they frantically tried to wrest control of their ships from the Corona. My voice cut through the turmoil.

"Gentlemen, I fear the worst has happened. This rebellion has contaminated the life source of the remaining Sirisians. I suggest we leave immediately with what we have. I will face the Igigi for my actions. Do it now."

A passionate but brief discussion followed. None could gainsay me. As Mission Commander, the decision, as well as the responsibility, belonged to me. We left the planet's orbit and laid in a course for Orpheus 2.

I did not waste any effort filing a report for the operation on Siris 7. I didn't see the need. I had no intention of being aboard ship when it left this system. I did, however, have one last task to complete before taking off the Corona. I called my clone. "Bathaal."

"Father, what has happened? The sky images are gone, and the attacker has been killed."

"Yes, but the danger has not passed. You must obey me, so listen closely. The others believe that that you and your followers are dead. Do nothing for one day. Tomorrow at this time, go up to the ship and speak this word, 'iftah.' The ramp will come down. Lead your followers inside. Your followers only! No others. Once inside you will find everyone in stasis. Speak this word, 'sakkri', and the ramp will retract, and the ship will depart. Do you understand? You must do exactly as I've told you. Your life depends on it."

"Yes, Father. Where?"

I hesitated. Loathe to share information as a general rule, I had to admit that Bathaal had opened my eyes. He had given me a chance to reclaim who and what I was. A Nephilim. That deserved more than harshness. I softened my tone. "It's a nice little planet. Much like Siris 7. It's called Damascus. Most importantly, it is not on any current charts or along any trade routes." *Because the Igigi stripped it bare centuries ago. And they never return to an empty planet.*

"Will you be with us?"

I ran through the plan in my head. Just before leaping into warp, I would board the escape pod. The disturbance caused by the warp signature of the five ships would hide me. From there it would be three dangerous days in the tiny pod before rendezvous with Marduk's ship.

"God willing."

"You have done well, Father. I look forward to seeing you on the Road to Damascus."

Lupe's Reunion

The large room radiated warmth, love, and affection. Ten-year old Lupe basked in its luxuriousness. The soothing voice of the Master of Ceremonies tickled her ears with a sense of giddiness.

"The Dilmun Chapter of the Society of Galactic Terrans extends its arms in a warm envelopment for its newest member, Lupe Martine. Lupe is an honored and cherished addition to our family. Join me in wishing her a long and loving time with us."

Deafening, heart-felt applause washed over Lupe as she rose from her seat. The warm flush rushing through her body gave her eyes a dreamy appearance. All was right with the Galaxy.

"Your scheduled time has expired."

The jarring voice of the computer shattered the illusion. Lupe's sense of belonging dissolved with the dispersion of the of the holographic pixilation, leaving her as empty as the dull, gray room crisscrossed with the silvery matrix grid.

"See the Program Administrator to schedule your next time slot. Thank you. We hope your session has been beneficial."

Lupe complained under her breath, "It was until it ended."

Her shoulders slumped as she walked toward the hatch of the hologram deck. Her long, black hair slid around her arms and covered her face, hiding her disappointment. Loneliness once again enveloped her world.

Living on the Dilmun Space Station took dedication, not an easy assignment an orphaned child. Her studies as a botanist kept her busy and filled her days, but when study periods ended, Lupe had nowhere to go and no one to take her there. She spent most of her time in the agri-pods and as comforting a presence as she found the plants, she could not accuse them of being brilliant conversationalists. She desperately wished for a friend, a playmate, and a sense of belonging.

"Grr. I should have scheduled back-to-back sessions. Next time I will."

Entering the outer corridor that encircled Dilmun, Lupe spied her guardian, Professor Mengel. For the past five years the slightly-built professor with the dark, penetrating eyes had served as the authority figure in her life. He guided her educational choices and served as her mentor but fell short of being parental. Lupe couldn't explain why, exactly, but the professor didn't generate any genuine warmth. Still, she loved him, at least as much as she knew how.

"Lupe! I'm glad I found you. I have good news."

"Good news? Really? Tell me Professor Mengel. Quickly!"

"I have received a correspondence from the Committee of Colony Selection."

Lupe waited impatiently for more. None forthcoming, she chided, "Professor, do not tease. Tell me?"

"You have been accepted."

"That is super nova! When? What position?"

Professor Mengel smiled and put his hand on Lupe's shoulder. "Botanist, junior level, on the Jamestown.

With the resilience possible only in a ten-year old, Lupe shed her earlier frustrations and clasped her hands, bouncing on her toes in joy. Her exclamations ran together in her hurry to express them. "Botanist. Oh, thank you, thank you! I can't believe it. It is an answer to my prayers. When do I report?"

"The crew is being assembled for training as we speak." Professor Mengel hesitated. His warm demeanor slipped a bit. "You report next lunar."

Lupe's exuberance drained off with the change in her guardian's voice. A note of concern entered her voice. "There's a 'but,' isn't there?"

The professor stared at Lupe. She couldn't decide whether his expression searched or probed.

"Nothing serious. However, since you are still a minor there is a requirement for parental permission to begin training."

"So, what's the problem? They know I'm an orphan." She shivered, not wanting to remember the awful day of the attack that claimed her mother and father's lives. "You'll sign for me, won't you? You're my guardian."

The whir of servos approached from around the curve of the corridor. With a quick intake of breath, Lupe flattened against the outside bulkhead. A cyborg with robotic legs, hips, and left arm and shoulder, came into view. Lupe kept as much distance between her and the cyborg as possible. Her attention never left the metal man.

"Do you still have nightmares?" asked the professor.

Lupe shuddered. She answered with a shaky voice. "Yes. I still see that metal man hitting my daddy. He caused the explosion that killed my momma."

"Do you remember anything after that?"

"No, Professor Mengel. The dreams always end right there."

The professor's eyes clouded.

His long face worried Lupe, as did his next words.

"I thought the dreams had subsided."

"They have," she said, giving quick assurance. "But I still don't like the metal men. That's not wrong is it?"

"No, child," said Mengel. His tone softened. "You do realize that there will be cyborgs on the Jamestown."

"I know, but I'm lots better."

"You are indeed. But don't get your hopes up too far."

Lupe's emotions bounced between assurance and alarm. She furrowed her brow, twirling a lock of hair around her forefinger. "What do you mean? I thought you said I was accepted. It won't be a problem."

"I hope not." Professor Mengel squat down to look at Lupe face-to-face. He grasped her shoulders. "Lupe, child, we found your father. He's alive."

Lupe's legs wobbled. She would have collapsed without the professor's support. After a couple of failed attempts, she managed, "My daddy?"

"Yes," said Professor Mengel. "As part of your application the Committee of Colony Selection ran a DNA check. They found your father. Somehow, in all the confusion after the incident, he was mistaken for another. He's been working as a deep space pilot for all these years."

"But ... but."

"It surprised him, too. He had no memory of the incident or his past. After the DNA match, Space Authority ran more tests. The results proved beyond doubt that Earnesto is your father."

Goosebumps rose on her arms.

"After being informed about you and your application, he wanted to talk to you. He will be here tomorrow."

Lupe's breath caught with an audible gasp. "He's coming here?"

"Yes, and he is excited to see you."

Lupe bounced on her toes, unable to contain her growing excitement. "My daddy's alive. What's he like? Have you seen him? Why didn't he visit? Wait, he didn't know. Oh, I'm so excited!"

"So is he or so I've been told," said Mengel. He smiled warmly. "You run along now. You are in no state to attend any classes. I've reserved more time for you on the holo-deck if you want it."

Lupe threw herself into Mengel's arms. She buried her face in his shoulder. "Thank you, Professor Mengel."

"You're welcome."

Lupe's thoughts whirled with visions of meeting her father. She couldn't concentrate on anything but the coming reunion. Soon, she found herself at the holo-deck. Unlike the other times, a contoured chair sat in the middle of the dull gray room. Upon it lay a tiara-shaped neural accentuator.

"Welcome, Lupe," intoned the computer. "Have a seat. What program would you like to run?"

Lupe shrugged. She didn't know of any programs in the computer's library that covered her current dilemma. "I don't know. Tomorrow I'm going to meet my father for the first time and I'm nervous."

"I have a program to relax you. Sit on the chair and lie back."

The computer's voice soothed Lupe's rising anxiety. She took her place on the chair.

"Are you comfortable?"

"Yes, I am."

"Put on the tiara and close your eyes. Imagine your father."

Lupe obeyed. A subtle vibration in the chair eased her tense muscles. Music enveloped her. A soft moan of contentment escaped Lupe's lips as she drifted off into sleep.

✶✶✶

THE SPARSELY POPULATED terminal area allowed Lupe an unimpeded view of the arrival airlock. She immediately recognized the handsome Latino man disembarking. She squealed in delight. "Daddy!"

Eyes bright and with a radiant smile, he went to a knee, opening his arms in welcome. "Lupe, my daughter. I am home. Come to me."

Lupe rushed into his embrace.

"I am so glad to see you," said her father, Earnesto. "I have thought of nothing but you for a long time. I'll never leave you alone again."

"I love you, Daddy."

"And I love you, baby."

Lupe had never been so happy. Not even before ... the incident ... could she remember being so content. The terminal area swirled in an eye-soothing sensory shift. The kaleidoscopic cloud departed with the light-stretching image of a warp drive. She found herself in the copilot seat of a colony scout ship.

Next to her sat Earnesto wearing a pilot suit with a sonic pistol strapped to his leg. Baldrics crisscrossed his chest in a dashing and adventuresome fashion. A lush blue-and-green planet filled the viewscreen on the control panel. White clouds swirled around in its atmosphere. Lupe had never seen a planet so beautiful. It perfectly reflected her contentment. She listened breathlessly as her father described his prior visit to the planet.

"We spent days exploring the dense foliage, searching for the beast."

"You knew it was the one that attacked the camp?"

"Yes," said Earnesto. "I tracked her myself, though I didn't know the creature was a she at the time. But I knew you were coming and I resolved that no danger would threaten my daughter."

Lupe swelled with pride. At this moment, she thought her father perfect in every way. He continued.

"We finally found her curled around her cubs in a patch of Nepeta Cataria."

Lupe gasped. She brought her hands up to cover her open mouth. "Ooh, cubs?"

Earnesto nodded. "Yes."

Alarmed at the seriousness of his of his voice, Lupe asked, "You didn't ...?"

"Kill them all?"

Lupe saw the amusement twinkling in his eye.

"No. I saw how harmless the plant made them, so I gathered up seeds and planted them around your work area. I won't have my daughter being in any kind of danger. Not ever again!"

Relieved that her father had not killed the cubs, her heart filled anew. "Oh, Daddy, I love you."

Earnesto wrapped his arms around Lupe. "And I love you, too, darling."

Lupe closed her eyes and fell into the closeness of the hug. When she opened them again, she found herself back on Dilmun Space Station sitting in the office of Mrs. Beatty, lead member of the Committee of Colony Selection. The stern demeanor of the bureaucrat enhanced the displeasure in her voice.

""You understand, Lupe, that when we selected you we thought you were an orphan. Now it seems you have a father. We are going to have to reconsider your appointment."

Lupe sat silent with her hands in her lap. She ducked her head to hide her disappointment. Her father's hand covered hers and gave them a squeeze.

"Mrs. Beatty," said Earnesto, "I have read over the requirements for your trip. I see where one of your shuttle pilots has withdrawn."

Mrs. Beatty's frown shifted from Lupe to Earnesto. "What are you suggesting, Mr. Martine?"

Lupe looked up at her father. Hope rekindled.

"You now have need of a shuttle pilot. My credentials are impeccable."

"I see," said Mrs. Beatty. "Very well, I'll have the contract drawn up."

Lupe clasped her father's hand tightly. "Daddy, you would volunteer to go just to be with me?"

"Of course, darling," said Earnesto. "Now that I have found you, I would move Heaven and Earth to stay by your side." Casting a quick glance in the direction of Mrs. Beatty, he leaned in closer to Lupe and whispered. "Or even a bureaucrat or two."

Tears threatened to spill over Lupe's eyelids. "Oh, Daddy, I love you."

Earnesto beamed. "And I love you, too, sweetheart."

A gentle alarm intruded on Lupe's moment. The soothing voice of the computer cut through Lupe's dreams.

"It is time to wake up. It is time to wake up. Your session is over. It is time to wake up."

Lupe opened her eyes. The program had seemed so real. She could still feel her father's strong arms around her. She looked around at the dull, gray room crisscrossed with a silvery matrix grid. A lazy smile stretched across her face. Happy and content, Lupe took off the tiara and returned to her room.

The next morning, well rested and eager, Lupe sat before Doctor Mengel's desk. Today she would reunite her father. She sat on the edge of her chair. Professor Mengel appeared reserved. *He has no reason to be excited. It's not his father that is returning.* She fidgeted, glancing back at the door.

"Are you ready, Lupe? At any moment your father will walk through that door."

"I'm very ready, Professor."

"What are going to do when you first see him?"

"I'm going to jump into his arms and hug him and hug him. It will be the happiest moment of my life."

The pneumatic door to Doctor Mengel's office hissed open. Lupe turned eagerly at the sound.

The strained whine of overstressed servos preceded the cyborg that walked into the office and stood next to Lupe's chair. The pong of unchanged hydraulic fluid overpowered the air scrubbers, compounding the uncomfortable silence.

Lupe fidgeted, trying to ignore the face which looked like a metallic mask.

Its lidless eyes glowed in a menacing manner. Hydraulic cylinders, driven by tiny servos rose from his trapezoids to his jaw, facilitating head and neck movement. Metallic parts replaced over half of the remainder of his body. It stood silent.

Lupe tried to look past the creature, back toward the door. Her attention darted about, searching adamantly for her father.

Doctor Mengel watched with interest while Lupe focus reluctantly settled on the cyborg.

"What is *that* doing here? Where is my Daddy?"

The cyborg turned in her direction.

"Hello, Lupe. You look exceptionally beautiful today. Just as I have imagined you."

Lupe screamed.

Doctor Mengel winced.

Her limp body hit the floor with a thud. Doctor Mengel cupped his chin with his right hand, his index finger stroking his cheek.

"She's feinted!" said Earnesto.

"So, she has."

"I thought you said you told her?"

"I did."

"I shouldn't have come," bemoaned Earnesto. "I should have let her continue to believe I died. This is all your fault!"

"Perhaps you are right."

Doctor Mengel sat up straight. He opened a side drawer in his desk and selected an electronic probe. "I believed her progress to be further along. The dreams had become so infrequent. I truly believed she was stronger."

"Well, what are you going to do? I must now live with this memory. And so does she."

"I can fix it. But first I shall take care of you."

Earnesto remained still as Doctor Mengel walked up behind him. The doctor waved a small scanner behind and above Earnesto's left ear. A panel opened and Mengel inserted his probe.

"I've thought about it," said Earnesto. "Now that I have seen her."

A series of soft beeps emitted from Mengel's probe.

"I don't want to fooorrrrrgggggggeettttttttt."

The electronics controlling voluntary brain functions powered down. The cyborg slumped forward and ceased movement. A series of blips and beeps accompanied Doctor Mengel's adjustments to Earnesto's memory banks.

"I'm afraid the choice is not yours to make. That should do it."

Doctor Mengel closed the panel on Earnesto's head. "Now for Lupe."

The doctor walked over to Lupe and lifted her from the floor. He carefully placed her on the couch against his office wall. He passed his scanner over the back of her head. The RF signal opened a panel revealing a sophisticated AI made from living tissue. The only one of its kind.

The long-ago explosion robbing Lupe of her parents had actually claimed three victims. Lupe's head injury had given Mengel the perfect opportunity at the perfect time. His breakthrough discovery needed a test subject and Lupe could be given a second chance. But, in order for the AI to be accurately assessed, the living subject had to be unaware of its existence.

Doctor Mengel's voice held a trace of sadness as he administered to Lupe. "I'm sorry, dear. I wish I could have told you long ago, but I thought your AI would integrate with your human psyche much better than this. I'll just erase this episode and we'll start again."

Day of Beginning

Ardashir tip-toed on egg shells. The day he waited forty years for had arrived. Today, he would be free of the compulsion. At this year's Day of Beginning pageant he would hand over responsibility of being First of the Republic of Koi to his son, Paiman.

"Paiman, come to the balcony," he called. "You do not want to miss the launch of the colony ships."

Ardashir tracked Paiman's progress by the swish of floor length robe. He pictured his son in the customary garb of the First; golden robe, red silk sash, and sandaled feet. Only the brightly colored, feathered headdress worn only by the Shaman, the First, distinguished father from son, at least on the surface.

Ardashir bore the signs of wearing the headdress. On occasion he had to remind himself to straighten his stooped shoulders. When he shaved in the morning, tired eyes, ready for release, stared back at him.

In comparison, Paiman's face shone with youthful vigor. Though his posture, however straight and tall, revealed a desire to be elsewhere. It saddened Ardashir to be the one to dash his son's plans.

"By day's end, Paiman, you will be the ruler of all this." Ardashir swept his arm across the vista before them.

To the south, the broad expanse of Urartu, Koi's capital city, clean and orderly, sparkled in the morning light. To the north sprawled the military run Academy of Knowledge where the colonists had trained for the last nine months. Before the two men, a spaceport dominated the large island in the middle of the river Majestic. Pointing upward like the three fingers of Ardashir's hand, the colony ships stood poised to launch the seed of humankind into the stars.

As if on cue, the first of the three ships, powered by newly designed gravity drives, lifted silently from the pad and arced into the sky. In quick succession, the other two followed. Ardashir missed the ponderous thunder and roar of the early vehicles clawing and fighting their way spaceward atop a blinding light. Back then, they shined like a beacon, visible for miles, demonstrating to all within sight the wisdom and might of the peoples of Koi. Of course, true wisdom resided in the use of engines that required no fuel. Still ....

Ardashir shook his head. Without the noise and light show, the lift-off seemed anti-climactic. He sighed. The compulsion within him eased somewhat. He knew it would not be completely dispelled until he passed his position to Paiman.

The history of the transference was as long as the line of Namtar, the Eldest, First of Firsts. More than tradition, the ritual survived unbroken since the first Coming of Age when Namtar witnessed the compulsion administered to his son, Jahangir. From that time forward, a son born to the First of the Republic on his thirtieth birthday, took up the burden of the compulsion.

"You must be excited, Paiman. Today is your Coming of Age. By this evening, you will be First of the Republic and President of the Koi Consortium."

Paiman showed no outward reaction.

He seldom does.

Paiman turned his head to look at his father. A slight upturning of the corner of his mouth revealed that he did feel some emotion. A gleam appeared in his eyes. "Are you that anxious to be done, Father?"

Deposing of decorum, as he was about the shed many more concerns, Ardashir put his arm around his son's shoulders and led him back into the office. "Truthfully? Yes, I am."

Paiman dipped his shoulder and Ardashir's arm slid off. "Then it will dishearten you to learn that I will not accept the position of First."

Ardashir ducked his head. He scrubbed his face to hide his disappointment. The pair crossed the office and entered the room reserved for receiving formal visitors. *I had hope it wouldn't come to this. Refusal only makes it harder. You will be First.*

Ardashir took his accustomed seat and indicated the one closest to him.

Paiman sat down.

"You are not the first to decline." *Nor was I.*

Paiman arched his eyebrows.

"I know you have been taught the history of Koi and the Firsts. As you can imagine, there is a version for public consumption and then there is what actually happened."

Paiman sat back in his seat, clearly uninterested.

"you are a dutiful son," said Ardashir with more hope than belief. He settled in his chair. "Two thousand, six hundred and thirty-seven years ago...."

THE CHILL BREEZE OFF the river made Namtar shiver despite the thick pelt of hair that grew over his entire body. He eyed the son, low to the horizon and with an orange tint. Soon it would sleep away the night in its bower. There would be no more heat until it woke and returned to the sky.

Namtar looked longingly across the river to the island. He wished he had a way to cross over. On the island, his people would be safe from the beasts that hunted at night. Namtar knew this would be so. Tearing his gaze away from the island and its promised safety, he straightened from his normally stooped posture and looked about for Sari, his mate. Gathering herbs and roots that grew along the river bank had taken her out of his sight.

A light in the darkening sky caught his attention. A shiver of premonition shook him. He sensed a strange occurrence in the offing. Namtar often watched the stars at night when he couldn't sleep. He knew the stars moved, but not like this one. It did not follow the rest in a slow, steady march across the sky or flash across in a bright streak. This one moved like the glow bugs of late spring and early summer, going here or there with no apparent purpose.

"Sari. Woman, where are you?"

Only the voices of the night bugs answered his call. Namtar kept his eyes on the light on the sky. It grew larger. Urgently, he called again. "Sari, come now."

"I am here, Namtar."

Namtar flinched. Sari stood next to him. He had not heard her approach.

"What are you looking at?" she asked.

Namtar shook his head. "I do not know."

Sari pulled on his shoulder. "You called. I am here. Let us get back to the people."

Namtar shrugged off her hand. The light mesmerized him, growing larger as it neared the spot where they stood.

"Namtar, why does that light in the sky move? Is that your fear? I am scared now. Let us go."

It was too late. Namtar stood like a statue, rooted to the spot. Moving faster than any object he had ever seen, the light flashed toward them before suddenly stopping and hovering directly over them. Through the brightness, Namtar could make out a dim shape. It reminded him of a large, round, flat boulder. A luminescent beam emitted from the bottom of the flying rock. It engulfed the pair.

The ground fell away. Seat beaded Namtar's forehead. He found no solid support beneath his feet. A scream welled up in his throat, but when he opened his mouth, nothing came out. He turned his head and saw Sari rising with him.

The light of the sun bathed the insides of Namtar's eyelids with a rosy glow. Opening his eyes, he had to blink several times to bring his vision into focus. He saw that the sun had roused and climbed back into the sky to watch over the people. *No, that's not right.* Namtar wasn't sure how he knew, but he did. The sun didn't move. The land did. He shook his head to clear his mind of those strange thoughts and looked around. Sari lay next to him in the grass. Her eyes fluttered open.

Namtar, what happened?"

Namtar thought back, trying to remember. Jumbled and confused, his thoughts refused to organize. He remembered some kind of hat on is head. Then a voice spoke within him. It told him how to put the plants they liked to eat into the ground instead of searching for them, how to make — Namtar's mind struggled to wrap itself around the foreign concept — tools. The voice told him how to cross the river. Most importantly, it told him to keep what happened secret. "I do not know, but we mustn't tell anyone. Not even your mother. Or that chatter-chatter friend of yours, Mina. You must swear."

"Not even Mina?"

"No! especially not Mina."

Namtar managed to wrangle a promise out of Sari. She swore, but Namtar had the feeling his mate left words unspoken.

"FATHER, ARE YOU SAYING that Namtar, First of Firsts, lacked basic humanoid knowledge before being abducted by extra-terrestrials?"

The shocked look of disbelief on Paiman's face reminded Ardashir of when his father told him the tale. He hadn't believed either. But that had been before ... Ardashir squashed the thought. He mustn't get ahead of himself. "No, what I am saying is that basic skills amounted to the extent of the Koi's knowledge. Pay attention and remember. One day you will tell this tale."

"Not likely," snorted Paiman.

After a brief glare, Ardashir resumed the telling. "Days became weeks, then months. Sari remained true to her word. Even after her pregnancy became obvious, she said nothing. Not even to Namtar, but he knew. The same something that changed his life had changed Sari's, too. He just didn't know how.

"Let me guess," said Paiman. "Aliens artificially inseminated her."

Ardashir remained calm. He took a deep breath and exhaled. "I almost prefer the silent son to the mocking one."

"I'm sorry, Father." Paiman had the dignity to look ashamed. After a pause, he asked, "What do you mean, almost?"

"Because of your passion, you will fight the truth all the harder. Then, after your conversion, you will pursue your compulsion with even greater vigor."

Paiman closed his eyes and shook his head.

Ardashir's sympathy grew. He really did want to be the one to inform Paiman. Becoming first meant becoming a Shaman and that required a certain surgical procedure. Painful enough for the willing, it could be even worse if unprepared. Ardashir loved his son and wanted to spare him as much as possible. He took up the story once again.

"You are correct. The Teachers artificially inseminated Sari using enhanced sperm from Namtar. They are very skilled."

"Father, please," said Paiman. "You are wasting your time. I have decided. I will not become First. You will not change my mind."

Tinged with sadness, Ardashir said, "No, son, I am not wasting my time. There is only one choice, made long ago. It lacks only fulfillment."

Ardashir reached up and took off his headdress, revealing the skullcap he wore underneath it. Then he reached up to remove the cap.

Paiman sat up in his chair. His eyes grew wide.

Ardashir never allowed anyone to see him bareheaded.

Paiman gasped. His wide-eyed look morphed into one of terror. Pale and shaken, he fell back in his chair. A perfectly symmetrical grid of receptacles protruded from Ardashir's skull. Tiny arcs of energy flickered among them.

"Voice-to-skull receptors. Through them I communicate with the Teachers. They are the ones that have been guiding the Koi all along. Jahangir, son of Namtar and Sari, served first. With the Koi, however, there is a limit as to how long our bodies will safely accept them. That limit is forty years. My time is over. Yours is about to begin."

Paiman's panic-filled eyes flicked rapidly back and forth, seeking escape. "No, no. It can't be true."

The sincerity and assuredness of Ardashir's tone reinforced the sympathy in his words. "At the moment, it doesn't matter whether you believe it or not. You will soon."

An otherworldly tone punctuated Ardashir's words. He gestured to a point behind his son. "Turn around. Say hello to Enki."

Paiman rose and turned slowly. A man a little taller than Paiman, slimmer, with dazzling bright blonde hair, stood waiting. The strange tone sounded again. A disturbance marred the air between the two. Two more men, similar in appearance to Enki, materialized.

Paiman stared, unmoving.

"Son, stand between those two men. No harm will come to you. The next phase of your Coming of Age is about to begin. You are about to become a Shaman. I will see you shortly to conclude the Day of Beginning celebration."

Paiman's body trembled. The two men stepped forward and assisted the terrified, but unresisting Paiman. The transporter activated, and the three men vanished.

Enki moved next to Ardashir's chair. The soon to be ex-First of Koi lifted his gaze to the Teacher. "You promised that Paiman would be the last. Is that still true?"

Enki's face took on a solemn expression, despite the grin flirting around the corners of his mouth. "Yes. Paiman's tenure will focus on preparing the Koi to join the Most High Federation of Planets."

Ardashir leaned his head against the chair back and took a deep breath, enjoying the sensation of warmth spreading through his body. "Our long journey is nearly over."

"And your next one is about to begin." He opened his hand. In his palm lay a data chip. "Remember this?"

Ardashir sat up straight. In a breathless voice, he said, "My authorization."

"Are you ready?"

Ardashir rose eagerly. Rejuvenation, the reward promised all of Koi's shamans, waited. Not only would he finally relinquish the compulsion, he would be made whole, his life spent in service to the Teachers renewed. He would have the body of a thirty-year-old again. "Is my father still aboard?

Enki smiled. "Yes, he awaits your arrival with keen anticipation."

Ardashir gazed at Enki through the sparkling mist of joyful tears. "Not to sound ungrateful, old friend, but I have been ready for some time now."

Farewell My Friends, Goodbye

MISSION ELAPSE TIME:
   7 DAYS: 22 HOURS: 13 MINUTES: 6 SECONDS

The Mars 1 escape capsule, a small part of a ship comprising an infinitesimally smaller speck in the enormity of space, limped toward Earth. Within it rode Lieutenant Commander Mark Steele and the ill-fated hopes of Space Authority's expansion to Mars.

"Mission Control, this is Mars 1. I don't know if you'll reach me in time or if my sub space transmitter has the range to get to Earth. It may be that you'll receive this after I'm ... well ... retrieved. This is my third day in the pod. Power levels are good. Target lock is strong. Oxygen levels are low. I'm initiating sleep mode for oxygen conservation. I expect to wake up at home."

If I wake up at all. Mark rubbed his hand over his stubbly scalp. He wanted to stretch cramped muscles, but being taller than most astronauts, he had even less room in the escape pod than most. With a bit of concern, Mark patted down his spacesuit.

"Where's the picture of my family?"

He unsealed a Velcro pocket and drew out a worn photograph. A warm wave of satisfaction spread through him. His face slowly stretched into a grin.

"Ah. Here it is."

He adhered the picture to the instrument panel before him. Mark tenderly caressed his wife's hair. "If you get to listen to this, Trixie, I love you, honey. Bobby, Sandi, I'll see you soon."

Mark closed his eyes. As he drifted off to oblivion, he prayed, "Be there for me, John. Help me expose Plish."

DREAMLAND: TWO MONTHS EARLIER

Mark put his phone down on his desk and massaged his temples. At thirty-six he should have been in his prime. Instead, crow's feet were already evident at the corners of his blue eyes. *The next thing you know I'll be losing muscle tone.* Mark had seen premature aging in other Astra pilots. The text he'd just received didn't strengthen him any. He was *not* looking forward to talking to Colonel Plish. He reread the message.

"Meet me in the hanger at 0930."

Col. Plish has discovered that Trixie is restoring my memories.

Why else call Mark in? Local commanders handled daily operations. Col. Maximillian Plish commanded Space Fleet. For him to speak directly to Mark meant something big. Mark didn't think it was to congratulate him for his promotion to Lieutenant Commander.

Mark looked at the clock on his phone. 0915. He rose to leave. He would rather have engaged a Draco patrol on the dark side of Mars while low on ammo. His chuckle was out of place considering his morose state, but Mark found it amusing that two years ago, he would not have been able to recall being on patrol. Trixie had saved him.

"You can't continue to undergo these mind wipes, Mark," Trixie had informed him after they returned from Stanford for the first time. "They're killing you."

At the time, Mark had just returned from a mission. He barely understood what his wife was saying. To keep her happy, he'd agreed to her treatments. Over time, snippets of conversations came back to him. He recalled radio chatter discussing the current allegiances with the aliens. He also recalled that after every mission, Col. Plish copied the memories of the TR-3B pilots and uploaded them into Space Fleet's massive AI. Mission memories were then replaced with canned recollections.

Mark now knew why. Plish couldn't have the truth of Space Fleet common knowledge. Not yet. It was too early. The Blue Avians and the Grays still opposed his proposed coup of the Terran government and the Draco's would see the disruption as an opportunity to attack. These memories made Mark a dangerous man to Plish. Now Plish wanted him.

How did I get caught?

Mark shook off the sensation of failure. How didn't really matter. Survival did.

The squadron ready vehicle took Mark to the hanger housing his Astra, Molon Labe. He stood before the postern recessed in the massive hanger door and looked at his watch. 0930. Suppressing the queasiness in the pit of his stomach, he punched his code into the security lock. The clunk of the titanium steel grips releasing the smaller entry sounded ominous. Mark hoped it wasn't a harbinger of things to come. Upon entering, Security, weapons leveled, surrounded him.

Out of the shadows stepped Col Plish. His starched uniform crackled with his movement. Shorter than Mark, and most everyone else, the colonel's presence towered over his subordinate. His short-cropped flattop, brown turning to gray, added to his no-nonsense bearing. Twin pools of depthless black with all the compassion of a soulless shark studied Mark. Their hardness bespoke of secrets and command.

"Congratulations on your promotion, Commander," he said with a disinterested voice, laden with accustomed authority.

A chilling wave swept over Mark, belying the colonel's superficial courtesy. It reminded him that this was not a social visit. "Thank you, sir."

At a nod from Plish, Security stepped away, their boots echoing in the cavernous space. "I brought you here to say goodbye to your bird," Plish said. "I understand you flyboys are sentimental about things like that."

Alarms clamored in Mark's mind. He could visualize the big screen's newest reincarnation of Robbie the Robot waving his arms and saying, "Danger. Danger, Will Robinson."

He attempted to play it off. "Why would I say goodbye?"

"Because you have requested a transfer to pilot NASA's Mars 1 mission. I have graciously approved it."

"I've done no such ...," Mark's denial died on his lips. He could see in the defiant posture of Col. Plish that the decision had already been made. There would be no altering course. "I see."

"I'm not sure that you do, Commander. You have put the Space Fleet at serious risk of disclosure. I have not spent my life putting this program together to protect our planet just to have you expose it simply to please your wife."

Mark squeezed down the bile that threatened to rise out of his stomach. *Does he also know of my plans?* Mark had discreetly hinted about the memory wipes with a few other Astra pilots. His Annapolis classmate, John Bonner, chief among them. *Has John been compromised?* "I don't know what you are talking about."

"Don't be coy, Commander. We found the traces of the chemicals used to preserve your memories. We know your wife, Trixie, received a PhD in neuro-chemistry from Stanford." Plish ticked off the points. "She reserved a lab and time slots for their MRI machine. Time slots that correspond with your down time. Did you think the Bay area was far enough away that we wouldn't find you? The Mars colony is not far enough away, Commander."

Mark could count his pulse from the pounding of the blood rushing through his burning ears. *If you or your goons did anything to Trixie and the kids....* His fingernails bit into his palm.

"Calm yourself, Commander. Other than this incident, you have a distinguished record. You may or may not remember, but your sortie against the Draco, T'Kar, and his clutch, demonstrated tactical brilliance. Your squadron drove them all the way into the asteroid belt. For that, I am willing to offer you a way out."

"Piloting the Mars 1 mission."

"Precisely."

"But that's a one-way flight. You've withheld shielding technology from the civilian space programs. Everyone in Space Fleet knows that."

"But not the public. You will be a hero," Plish raised a finger to forestall Mark's interruption, "and I will generously spare your wife and children."

Bullshit! "How do I know you will keep your word?"

"You don't. So, what's it going to be? Are you going to pilot the Mars 1 mission, or will you and your family disappear from the face of the Earth?"

Security returned. They charged their weapons.

The solid sensation beneath his feet disappeared. It was like an EVA without a tether. Fear welled up within him, bringing with it the crushing shame of defeat. *Do I make Trixie a widow now or in a few weeks?* The saliva in his mouth soured. It took every ounce of willpower he had not to lunge at Plish and damn the consequences. "I'll fly it."

TWO DAYS BEFORE LIFTOFF: FAMCAMP, EDWARDS AIR FORCE BASE

The aroma of hamburgers, chicken, and brats cooking on the numerous grills fired up for the pre-launch party did little to cheer Mark. Not even the yells and screams of the horde of astronaut children at play, usually a sure-fire smile bringer, alleviated Mark's downer mood.

"Your time's coming. I know it."

The words rang hollow in Mark's ears even as he said them. His delivery wasn't getting any better with practice. The young woman walked away with a determined step. Mark wiped his palm on his pant leg, trying to scrub off his insincerity.

He shook his head. The civilian astronauts just didn't get it. How could they? They thought they existed on the cutting edge of exploration. If they knew that Mark had flown missions beyond their dreams, that Space Fleet freighters routinely flew to Mars servicing secret Martian bases, they would be seething with envy, not offering platitudes and false encouragement. But Space Fleet was a secret and would remain so until Plish finished building his empire. Mark planned to do something about that.

He returned to Trixie and sat down at the picnic table. "I'll be glad when this is over."

"Mark!"

Mark glanced at Trixie. "Is Michelle with him?"

"Just John," Trixie said.

Mark wondered if Trixie intentionally punned him. Early on, she had lobbied hard to bring the Bonners into the escape plan. Mark had mentioned the memory wipes to John as a possible source of the mission lag they all suffered from, but refused to involve him or any of the pilots from the White Hat squadron in his planned disclosure of the Space Fleet. He deemed enlarging the cabal too risky. He needed John and the White Hat's help to look spontaneous.

Mark turned around and stood up. "John, I've been trying to reach you."

"So I heard. Let me shake your hand. Piloting the Mars mission. That's got to be exciting." He leaned in and whispered, "It's not too late. I've got a vial. Measles. It'll knock you down for three days, then it's gone."

"What else did Trixie give you?"

John backed away, hands raised. "Hey, what makes you think it was Trixie? You taught the White Hats to be resourceful." John kept his voice low. "Astras have Disruptors, Mark. The Civvies don't even know they need one."

"I know."

"That bus you'll be flying doesn't maneuver for shit. If you encounter a solar flare once you get past the Van Allen Belt, you're toast, and you know it. Don't be his martyr."

"And ending up a brain-dead zombie is better, how?"

John ducked his head.

Mark put his hand on John's shoulder and gave it a squeeze. He wasn't proud of brow-beating his friend. Especially since what John said was true. The TR-3B's Mercury plasma accelerator ring, a.k.a. magnetic field disruptor, rotated at 60,000 RPM at 250,000 atmospheres. It enveloped the craft in a magnetic layer of plasma that not only reduced the weight of everything inside the layer by 89%, it also protected the crew from solar radiation.

Mark would have the benefit of none of that, but he didn't expect to need it. He did however need John and the White Hats. "There is something you can do."

"Yeah?" John arched a brow and said around a grin, "Name it."

"Monitor NASA's radio freqs. Space geeks do it all the time. Use them. Have Michelle and the other spouses listen from home, too. If I need a lifeline, raise a stink. Make them rescue me."

John's second brow raised to match the first. His eyes darted back and forth as if looking for an eavesdropper or one of Plish's stooges. "You going to sabotage the Mars 1?"

"Not me. Plish."

John looked confused. "Man, what did you do?"

Mark extended his hand, clasping John's. "Thanks for stopping by, John. I know I can count on you. And the White Hats."

John nodded and walked away.

Mark rejoined Trixie.

"If you'd recruited him like I suggested, you wouldn't have to be covert," she said.

"If I recruited him like you suggested, then there would be two pilots on the Mars 1 mission."

"You don't know that."

"Don't start."

Anger flashed in her eyes. "I can't help it! I'm afraid."

Mark stood and walked around the table. He gathered Trixie up in his arms. Even through her summer clothing, he felt her heart pounding against his chest. He clasped her tighter and cooed," Everything will work out. I'll make it back."

"But what if you don't," she sobbed.

Mark pushed himself gently away. Reaching into his pocket he pulled out a triangular token. Trixie had found it under her plate the night Mark had taken her out for a celebratory meal after accepting the offer from Plish to fly Astras. It had been the first indication of what he had gotten them into.

He moved the disc until the holographic image of Plish appeared. At the time, Mark hadn't told her the identity of the man on the disc. "If I don't come back or if I come back a vegetable and you see this man, take the kids and get as far away from him as possible."

Trixie lifted tear-filled eyes from the image. "That's him, isn't it?"

"Yes. That is Colonel Plish. Do not interact with him. Flee. The publicity will die down after a while. Come get me then."

Trixie took the disc. She blinked her red, puffy eyelids.

It tore at Mark's heart strings to see tears leaving wet, mascara-infused streaks down her cheeks. He had never seen her so beautiful

Trixie choked back a sob. "If need be, I'll find you. If there's anything left, I'll restore it."

Mark wondered if he'd see her again after tomorrow. He crushed his lips against hers.

MISSION ELAPSE TIME:

3 DAYS: 37 MINUTES: 16 SECONDS

For the first three days *Mars 1* operated perfectly. A fact Mission Control constantly reminded Mark of as they reported his blood pressure readouts. Their admonishments to calm down or relax achieved little success. Mark felt like a powder keg too near the fire.

He saw every incident as a potential catastrophe. He'd expected his shuttle to explode on liftoff. After joining the *Mars 1* parked in orbit, he looked for a catastrophic failure on the ship's initial burn. With every course correction, Mark's breath caught in his throat anticipating electrical arcs between navigation and thruster relays or, even worse, nothing happening at all. No engine burn, nothing. For three days, he existed on the razor's edge.

Since he woke on the third morning, the radio tuner drifted, unable to lock on a frequency, a power fluctuation developed in the command module generating sudden surges that knock critical systems offline, and now this.

Mark slapped his palm against the outer edge of the long-range radar display. It failed to fix the problem. "Damn you, Plish!" Mark unhooked his tether while he groused, "And of course, the backup instrument panel is in the last module."

At least the nausea of zero gee had finally subsided and Mark had stopped bumping into every protruding sharp object. As he pulled himself through the science module, the second of four docked together along the central spine of *Mars* 1, Mark longed for the crewed compartments of Astras which maintained standard Earth gravity. In fact, on board the TR-3bs there was no indication of motion at all. He could go lightspeed in one direction and in a nan-second be travelling at lightspeed in the opposite direction without experiencing any of the effects of Newton's Law of Motion. Making Earth's Space Authority reinvent the wheel for every aspect of space flight must have amused Plish. Mark wondered if the Colonel monitored *Mars 1* with glee.

"First the radio, then the solar array, now the radar. What the hell else have you got in store for me, Plish?"

Mark had taken to talking to himself since he boarded *Mars* 1. He found the sound of his voice preferable to silence. It also complimented the blaring alarms so well.

Entering the third module, a flashing alarm caught his attention. Mainly housing the galley and exercise equipment, the third module also contained the escape pod. Mark floated over to read the display.

"You have exceeded the programed parameters to return to Earth. Do you wish to delete this message?"

Mark clenched his jaw, biting back the string of obscenities that readily came to mind. He had pre-programmed the escape pod. This message was a reminder that every moment more he spent on this mission decreased his chances of survival. It also served as an indicator of how large a threat Plish considered him. He had waited until Earth was beyond range of *Mars 1* escape pod to sabotage the mission. Any hope Mark had of surviving now rested with his wild card, John Bonner.

"*Mars 1,* Houston."

Mark pressed his earpiece further into his ear, straining to hear through the heavy static. "Go ahead, Houston."

"Radar is picking up some incoming targets at your two o'clock. Do you have visual?"

Targets? Mark spun around, looking for his tactical display. Too late, he realized he wasn't aboard the *Molon Labe*. The energy of his spin drove his head forcefully against the escape pod hatch. "Ow! Dammit. Are they Dracos?"

"Say again, Mars 1."

"Nothing. What kind of targets?"

"A small swarm of asteroids."

Mark recognized his opportunity. He silenced the alarm and made his way back to the command module. "That's a negative on the visual, Houston. What is their trajectory?"

"We're calculating trajectory now, Mars 1. Standby."

"Standby's ass," Mark muttered under his breath. Faint staccato *tinks* peppered his spacecraft. It sounded like a shotgun fired in a tin barn. "Houston, I'm being struck by debris. It's too small to be picked up on short-range radar."

"Roger that, Mars 1. Turn ten degrees to port."

"Ten degrees to port, roger."

Mark knew designers had not engineered *Mars 1* to withstand an encounter with even a small asteroid swarm. A blip suddenly appeared on the radar screen, heading directly toward him. Displays indicated a target about the size of a shoebox. Mark moved the control stick to starboard, providing the rock the largest possible target away from the escape pod. He unhooked his harness and launched himself back to the escape pod.

WHUMP.

Collision alarms blared. He bounced of the hatch between the second and third module. His focus sharpened as an increase in adrenaline flooded his blood stream. The capsule plunged into darkness. Mark heard the hiss of escaping oxygen.

A warm glow of satisfaction settled in his stomach. The collision, while fatal to the *Mars 1* mission, had not been catastrophic to Mark, yet. Now to convince Houston and the thousands that monitored every NASA mission on various social media platforms, to rescue him. *I hope you are listening, John.*

"That one hurt, Houston. Thrusters off-line. Power levels dropping. Switching to backup. I've lost the stick, Control. I say again, I've lost the stick. I cannot maneuver."

The ship yawed. Without thrusters the yaw would become a tumbling spin. *Get in the escape pod.*

The backup power source hummed to life. Illumination returned. He called Mission Control. "Houston, backup power is on. Still no joy on the stick. Suggestions?"

"We're working on it, Mark."

Mark sealed the pod's hatch. "I'm outta time, Houston. I'm punching out."

"You're too far away from Earth for the escape pod."

"Then throw me a lifeline."

Sweat beaded Mark's forehead. Everything had come down to this. Thanks to the delays early in the mission, there was not enough oxygen in the escape pod's tank to reach Earth. Even if there was, the pod would not survive reentry. Space Fleet would have to bring him home. John had the duty, but would he break off his patrol to rescue Mark?

The ejection of the pod forced Mark back into his cushioned chair. Through his viewscreen he saw a rock as big as a motorcycle smash into *Mars 1*. Seconds later a shock wave rocked the escape pod. *Mars 1* was space debris.

PRESENT DAY: EARTH

Rhythmic blips and beeps sang a song of sorrow, bitter and sharp like the smell of the astringents and disinfectants in the air. Or so it seemed to Colonel Plish. Mark lived.

Across the room, sedated and secured to his bed by straps, Mark lay in a semi-conscious state. One stand, next to the head of his bed, held a group of monitors displaying his vitals. On the other side, several tubes ran into a saline drip and then down to an IV delivering Mark's memories for recording. Plish sat in a chair by the door with his back to the wall, sorting the situation. "Bonner's a fool! I'll reassign him to the Martian Squadron. I've never liked the smell of hospitals."

A single auxcable ran from the helmet that covered Mark's eyes and ears to a laptop. Plish's aide did not look away from the recording. "No, sir."

"And I don't like insubordination. It's a virus. It must be eliminated."

"Yes, sir."

"I want you to disband those White Hats. No, wait. That'll spread the poison. Leave them all together, they'll be easier to watch. Except Bonner."

The aide rose from his stool. He strolled across the room and handed Plish a triangular disc.

"How is he?

"Stable," said the aide. "Here is the recording you asked for."

"Too bad. I'm almost tempted to terminate him."

"Just give the word."

Plish leaned his elbows on the arm of his chair and fisted his palm over and over. "If he dies, that blowhard from the watchdog group will blame the President. The Press hates the President so much they'll run with it. Next thing you know there will be Congressional investigations. No. Let him live. Have one of our doctors give a presser. The mob will follow the next shiny new thing that comes by." Plish rose from his chair. "Leave little more than a shell."

"Yes, sir."

"I'll salvage this and then use it as proof to convince the Blue Avians that I have compassion."

TRIXIE WAITED WITH hopeful expectation. Her friend Michelle Bonner, supervisor of nurses, had told her last night that Mark had been transferred to this room. The door to Mark's private room opened. Her heart lurched. *It's him! The face on the disc.* His eyes locked onto her. They were the eyes of a merciless predator. She clasped her hands together to keep them from trembling.

"Mrs. Steele?"

Trixie nodded, too afraid to ask how he knew.

"Please, walk with me," said Colonel Plish.

Flee. Don't engage. Trixie fell in next to him.

Plish led her toward the exit. "Let me start by saying your husband is alive and stable."

Don't let on you know. "Are you his doctor?"

"Yes. I assume you watched the telecasts?"

"Yes, I did."

"I'm afraid the newscasters were correct. His escape pod ran out of oxygen before we could rescue him."

Trixie ducked her head to hide her disbelief. She couldn't prove it, but she knew Plish was lying.

"Your husband suffered oxygen deprivation. He had put himself into a deep sleep, but it wasn't enough. I'm afraid he has suffered memory loss."

Don't engage. Flee. Tears welled up. Trixie pushed them back down. She couldn't afford to break down. She took a deep breath and exhaled. "How much?"

"We don't know yet. We hope it is minimal. His quick action saved his life."

Our quick action, you mean. While refusing to be interviewed, Trixie had played a major role behind the scenes briefing and coaching those that did face the reporters. She glanced back up the hallway. She wanted to see Mark. It might be her last opportunity.

"We'll keep him for a few more days," said Colonel Plish, positioning his body as a barrier to prevent Trixie from returning to Mark's room. "You'll be able to see him then."

The publicity will die down. Come to me then. Those had been Mark's words. *Accept defeat for now. Live to fight another day.* Trixie nodded. "I see. Thank you, Doctor. Thank you for telling me."

Inside, she both shivered in fear and boiled with rage. She left the hospital and returned home to gather up the kids.

Trial by Demon

"M-m-m," purred Angeline.

The futon creaked with the shifting of her weight. Angeline's athletic body snuggled deep within the grasp of Malcolm's strong inviting arms. All was right in the Central Lands.

Malcolm's dreamy voice sank Angeline further into her contentment. "What's got you so intent?"

She murmured, "I just can't believe it."

"That we're betrothed?" said Malcolm.

Angeline's pleasure-fogged brain found the question confusing. *Of course, we're betrothed,* Angeline reasoned. *We've been promised since birth. The good news is that I was given Ambrosia!*

But one didn't speak aloud of magic to Malcolm. He resented that, Tierra, Goddess of the Central Lands and giver of magic, was the last of the three goddesses to rise. He resented Central Lander sorcerers and sorceresses being generations behind the East and West in skill. Most of all, he resented not being chosen as a magic wielder. Talk of magic in Malcolm's presence triggered distrust and ill-will.

She danced around the subject. "Well, that too and the High Priestess said that I have promise."

Before Malcolm could answer, the frantic voice of Baron Hap Simon echoed through the third floor of the manor. "Angeline! Angeline, where are you?"

Angeline and Malcolm disentangled themselves and sat up.

Angeline called out, "On the balcony, Father." She hissed at Malcolm, "Stand up. Straighten your clothes."

Hurried footsteps preceded Hap's entry. By the time he stepped through the double doors, Angeline had adjusted her damask pelisse, a short coat-like garment worn over her chemise, into something reasonably presentable. She needn't have bothered.

Her father's attention centered solely on his news. "Malcolm, you're here. Good."

Malcolm smiled, but there was no visible warmth behind it.

Hap, a slight man and easily agitated, paused. He leaned forward, putting his hands on his knees, and took several deep breaths. Once sufficiently oxygenated, he straightened and ran his fingers through his thinning, disheveled gray hair. "Your father, the Cap Tan, has been murdered."

Angeline inhaled sharply.

Malcolm bolted toward the door. "Murdered? By whom?"

Hap stepped in front of Malcolm. He held out his hands to stop him.

The two collided. Malcolm grabbed the little man to keep him from falling.

"Baron Yakov," said Hap. "He is trying to usurp the throne."

Malcolm tried to let Hap go, but he little baron clung to his future son-in-law as if he were a lifeline.

"There are too many of his men," protested Hap.

Angeline touched Malcolm's shoulder. "I'll use my sight. Maybe we'll see or hear something we can use."

Malcolm jerked his head around to stare at Angeline. His eyes blazed.

Angeline nodded, encouraging Malcolm to accept her suggestion.

He swelled up.

Angeline braced herself for his outburst.

Instead, he released Hap and walked away from them both. "Hurry. I'll be on the balcony."

Angeline heard the hurt in his voice. Wanting to ease it, she reached for the crystal pendant at her neck. A deathbed gift from her mother, the pendant marked Angeline as a sorceress. Her fingers closed around a metal cylinder.

A spark of pride left a warm glow in her stomach. Ambrosia. El-lina, High Priestess of sorcerers and sorceresses, didn't give a rare and powerful graduation token to just anyone. However, it wasn't what she needed. She released it and grasped her pendant. Closing her eyes, she concentrated on Chet Sinclair, Malcolm's father, the former Cap Tan of the Central Lands.

The sudden smell of cinnamon distracted her. A grunt of surprise from Malcolm drew her gaze toward the balcony. She caught a glimpse of a demon, red and hideous, with its arms wrapped around Malcolm. In a blinding flash, both disappeared. Angeline gasped, and froze. Her pendant fell from unfeeling fingers.

"What was that?" stammered Hap.

Angeline trembled. *What happened to Malcolm?* "I ... I don't know. I think, a demon."

"What's a Westerner doing here?"

"And what does he want with Malcolm?"

"This is not good," said Hap. He wrung his hands. "First the Cap Tan. Now Malcolm. Something's going on. Something big, but what?"

Angeline's mind raced from question to question. Kidnap, assassination, a coup ... why? *Calm down. One question at a time. Who has the answers?* High Priestess El-lina. If Angeline hurried, she could still catch her teacher before the Eastern Priestess returned to her home.

Out of the corner of her eye, a hand wave from behind her wardrobe. *What's he doing here?*

She gave her father a quick hug then pulled away. "I'll get to the bottom of this, Poppa," she said, shooing him away. "I'll report to the High Priestess. She'll know what to make of it. You get back to Uncle Marcus. You two need to hold the throne. I'm sure he needs you. And tell no one of the demon. There's no need for panic."

"Yes, yes, you're right." Hap released Angeline. He glanced at the balcony where the demon had been. "You be careful."

Angeline smiled in assurance, "I will, Poppa. I promise."

As soon as Hap left the room, Conner popped out from behind the wardrobe. Not many Central Landers had a Reek as a BFF, at least Conner considered himself Angeline's BFF. Angeline considered him a nuisance.

An attaché of El-lina, the small and impish Easterner had the strength of two men and the wit of none. On the upside, he could access an arsenal out of thin air. Angeline would have thought that strange, but her studies as a sorceress had taught her that, unlike Central Landers, all Easterners possessed magic of some sort.

"Are you really going to be careful?" Conner asked.

"Of course not. High Priestess El-lina says I have promise," declared Angeline. "Now I'm in a hurry, why are you in my rooms? Were you spying on me, peeker?"

"No, mistress. Conner wouldn't do that. Were you doing something worth peeking?"

Angeline ignored the question, her mind jumping to another conclusion. "Did the High priestess send you?"

"No."

She narrowed her eyes to slits. "How long have you been here? What did you see?"

"Much and little."

Angeline started forward.

Conner skipped away. "I saw the new Cap Tan enter, but not leave." He lowered his voice and touched his nose. "I smell demon."

Angeline raised her index finger to her lips. "Sh-h-h. Keep that to yourself."

Conner crept closer. He whispered, "Doirbhall wants you. She says now."

"Doirbhall?" Angeline put her fingers to her temple and grimaced. As if she didn't have enough troubles. She looked up and raised her hands, beseeching, "What else?"

—————————

ANGELINE SET A BRISK pace. The visiting quarters of the Simon family were two mansions east of High City Manor. To avoid any possible contact with Baron Yakov's men, Angeline traveled north past two residences before turning west to Sinclair Boulevard, the main thoroughfare leading from High City Manor. Doirbhall's shop was a few buildings ahead.

The herbalist claimed her shop's location the best in all High City, spacious, airy, and clean. Best of all, it was next to the Bursary, home of the Cap Tan's tax collectors. Central Landers stopped in before going to the Bursar to purchase charms for the bureaucrats to believe them. Those who didn't, came afterwards to purchase curses.

Charms aside, Angeline wondered what kind of business now involved her. Demons couldn't teleport far. Which meant the demon that snatched Malcolm stayed within a turning of High City, two if the demon was exceptionally strong. But why did a demon snatch Malcolm? If Malcolm died, the Central lands would lose its Cap Tan. "And I won't get married." Events had moved so quickly Angeline hadn't had time to fully consider all the ramifications. She could become a widow, before she ever married. She stopped abruptly. "Oh!"

Conner stumbled into her back. He spun around, a nocked bow materializing in his hand. He looked about for an adversary.

"My betrothed!" exclaimed Angeline. "The demon kidnapped my betrothed."

"Is that a normal custom, Mistress?" asked Conner.

Angeline spun around to face the Reek. She crossed her arms. "Are you eavesdropping?"

Conner scanned right, then left. "Conner didn't drop no eaves." He cocked his head up at Angeline. "So, do you rescue him now to prove your worth?" He squatted down, enraptured. "Conner thinks that is a good custom."

Angeline glared. It was bad enough being summoned by Doirbhall, she didn't need some half-wit from the Eastern Lands underfoot. "Why are you following me? You have delivered your message." She waved him away. "Go on now. Shoo."

Angeline started back up the boulevard. She heard the prancing steps of Conner behind her, along with his commentary.

"Such a nice custom. So romantic."

Angeline shook her head. A niggling thought crossed her mind. *Will El-lina send* me *after Malcolm?* The young sorceress visualized a confrontation between herself and a demon, her first trial as a sorceress. In an epic battle of strength and wit, she smote the Western creature who then groveled at her feet. Buoyed by her abundant self-confidence, she squared her shoulders and walked proud. She'd save Malcolm and pity the demon standing in her way. *Bring it.*

Angeline mounted the stoop to Doirbhall's shop. Like all buildings in High City, it consisted of a wood interior covered with a stone veneer to protect it from the harvest storms' lightning. Angeline reached for the bell rope. Her hand stopped halfway.

Doirbhall did not always exhibit the strongest support for Angeline and Conner had not said what the herbalist wanted with her. Angeline's earlier exuberance and confidence deserted her. She wondered if a storm awaited her inside and if she would need a protective veneer. The door opened.

"Come in, dear. Don't linger on the stoop. It looks indecisive. In with you, now."

A white headband smudged with residue from her herbal concoctions held Doirbhall's earthy red hair held off her forehead. She waved her pestle like a pointer. "What took you so long?"

Angeline stepped through the door. The interior of the shop reminded her of a giant web. Rows of shelving filled with all manner of jars, figurines, and ready-made charms radiated out from a counter in the center. Angeline always expected to see bunches of drying herbs tied to the rafters, but the shelves were orderly and the aisles clear. Scents of ginseng, licorice, and reishi tickled her nostrils. She sneezed. "My father stopped by. The Cap Tan has been murdered."

Doirbhall paused. She set her pestle in the mortar and wiped her hand on her bibbed apron before starting toward the counter at the center of the shop. "Who did it?"

Angeline followed Doirbhall up the aisle. "Baron Yakov. At least according to my father."

Doirbhall, pestle once again in hand, demanded, "What else?"

Why does she always interrogate me? Angeline resented the relentless questioning. Her thoughts scattered. "A demon kidnapped Malcolm from my balcony. Oh, and he proposed. We're now betrothed."

"You're betrothed to a demon?" Doirbhall glanced back at Angeline. "How inconvenient."

Mortified, Angeline's back arched in righteous indignation. Only the hours spent on footwork during sword practice kept her tangled feet from pitching her forward onto her face.

Reaching the counter, Doirbhall turned and faced her. The flicker of a smile on the herbalist's face prevented Angeline from making a bigger fool of herself. The smile didn't last long. With a stern look, she said, "You should have told me that first. Magic is involved and that concerns you. What are you going to do?"

"I'm on my way to El-lina."

"Then you will have to go all the way to Celeste City. She went home to the Eastern Lands."

Angeline's hastily made non-plan crumbled. "Already?"

Doirbhall nodded.

Now what am I going to do?

As if reading Angeline's mind, Doirbhall asked, "Now what are you going to do?"

"Baron Yakov kills the Cap Tan, disrupting the leadership of the Central Lands. A demon takes advantage and kidnaps Malcolm. There must be a connection."

Doirbhall stood before her, arms crossed, pestle in hand. "Well?"

It irritated Angeline that Doirbhall made her think. The High Priestess thought highly of Angeline. Why didn't the herbalist? Angeline could see only one truth. "A demon cannot be allowed to operate this close to High City."

Doirbhall pressed harder. "Go on."

Angeline sagged. She wondered what the harridan sought. A flash of inspiration brought clarity. "The Sunfather of the West stretches forth his hand. The Central Lands tremble."

"Mieze's Manifesto. You know it. Good girl. Tell me what I want to hear."

"You found a patron at Reis' manor!"

"You wish."

Reis's manor lay as far away from High City as one could get without going to Grimval valley. Angeline sighed. She couldn't win against Doirbhall. She thought harder. The pieces fell together. "You think the Cap Tan's murder and Malcolm's kidnapping is part of Mieze's Manifesto."

"Throw the lands into chaos, then invade."

A coldness developed in the pit of Angeline's stomach. Becoming a vassal to the Western Lands meant oppression. She had no desire to live in servitude. "The Sunfather must be stopped."

"What's the response to Mieze's Manifesto?"

Angeline responded by rote. "The smallest of seeds arise in the Central Lands. She causes the trembling to cease." Angeline paused. "Hey, what are you saying?" She glared at the herbalist. "The smallest of seeds? Really?"

"You're not done trembling, yet," said Doirbhall.

Angeline rolled her eyes.

Doirbhall set her mortar and pestle on the counter. She wiped her hands on her apron, paused, then snapped her fingers. "Yes, that should do it."

Angeline tracked the top of the healer's head as disappeared down an aisle on her left and returned.

"You need something to stop the trembling."

Angeline's senses heightened as she stared at a crudely shaped stone woman in Doirbhall's hand. She reminded herself to breathe. "That will stop it?"

"Not unless you throw it at the demon and, by good fortune, strike a vulnerable area. Use all of your senses, girl!" Doirbhall put the figurine in her mortar and crushed it into powder with a few strokes of her pestle. "Do not let your eyes dominate your thought."

Angeline clenched her jaw, biting back her acerbic response. Just once, she would like to have a pleasant conversation with the herbalist.

"Did you catch the demon's scent?" asked Doirbhall.

"Cinnamon."

Doirbhall frowned. "De Spar."

The hair on Angeline's arms stood up. Her skin tingled. The average Central landers' knowledge of the West may have been sketchy, but all sorcerers and sorceresses learned of De Spar, third in line behind the Sunfather of the West. Everything she ever heard about him ended in doom.

Doirbhall pointed her pestle at the metal cylinder hanging from a chain around Angeline's neck. "Give me your Ambrosia."

"I beg your pardon."

One did not simply hand Ambrosia over to another. Then again, Doirbhall wasn't just another. She was ... well, she was Doirbhall, trusted advisor to both El-lina and the goddess Tierra. Angeline unclasped the chain around her neck and handed the healer her graduation token.

Doirbhall opened the cylinder and set it on the counter.

Honeyed fragrance tickled Angeline's nostrils. Her mouth watered. Her fingers tingled with the need to touch the intoxicating substance. Doirbhall sprinkled a pinch of the ground figurine over her treasure. Angeline reached involuntarily for the cylinder.

"Have you located the demon yet?" asked the herbalist.

The healer's words grated against Angeline's ears, harsh and threatening. Her hands stopped short of the Ambrosia. She blinked rapidly and shook her head. What had Doirbhall asked? *The demon?* Clarity of thought returned. "He's close. That's all I know."

"We need more specifics. You haven't got all turning, girl. An idle mind's a demon's playground."

Angeline's cheeks reddened. She brought the cinnamon scent to mind. *Find.* She smelled the pungent aroma of rosemary, as her own magic followed the lingering traces of the demon's magic to its source and back. "He's less than a turning south, in the grasslands."

"Hmm, that would be the shrine of the Sisters of the Forlorn. Here," Doirbhall handed Angeline her cylinder. "It'll work only for a short time."

Angeline fastened the fine chain around her neck. "What will it do?"

Doirbhall smiled. "Possibly enhance an already unpleasant surprise in store for De Spar. Used properly, it stops the Central Lands from trembling. Now, off with you."

Unsatisfied, and feeling rushed, Angeline turned to leave.

Doirbhall gave a last farewell. "El-lina is right. You show much promise."

Outside, Angeline made her way down the boulevard to her father's manor. While pleased to receive the rare compliment from Doirbhall, she grumped, "She could speak more plainly."

Behind her, familiar steps approached.

"When are we leaving?" asked Conner.

Angeline didn't bother to look back. "Who are you and why are you talking to me."

"It's so romantic," said Conner, talking aloud to himself. "I must help the mistress. She'll need me."

Angeline spun around, intent on squashing any pretense he had of joining her. His face, the picture of innocence, stopped her. She chewed on her lower lip. A pang of regret over all the harsh words she had spoken to him pricked her conscience. De Spar brought death and Angeline didn't want to endanger her friend, but she could not deny the possibility of needing help. Only Conner stood by her side.

Since the rise of Tierra, De Spar had tripled his raids on the western border. The battle at Fourth Stone Fort had been particularly gruesome. Un Tier, ogre-like semi-humans had battered down the fort walls. After sacking the fort, they left behind a table laded with a sumptuous feast. Roasted Central Lander ribs, stews made with arms and thighs, and the fort's commander dressed and spitted over a fire welcomed the late-arriving reinforcements.

Many of the Central Land's newly discovered sorcerers and sorceresses had cried out to confront him, Angeline the most outspoken. El-lina warned Angeline against facing the Western demon.

"He is diabolical and ambitious. You are young and untried."

"Tierra's magic is pure and strong."

"It is only as pure and strong as the one wielding it."

"But you said I was the best in the Central lands."

"I said you showed a lot of promise, seedling. Go up against De Spar and that promise could be unrooted."

Now De Spar had her betrothed and El-lina could not help. Angeline, the smallest of seeds, faced her greatest trial. *I hope I'm strong enough.* For Malcolm's sake, and Conner's, Angeline had to be.

BY NOON THE NEXT TURNING, Angeline and Conner stood at the entrance to the hidden valley in the grasslands. In the center of the gently sloping plain rose the shrine of the Sisters of the Forlorn. Once a mill that ground flour for early transient monks seeking their place in the order of all things, the simple two-story dwelling had been maintained by the women and few spouses who stayed behind when the monks left. Stained glass replaced the previous plain windows and the large river wheel had been dismantled. In its place, flues provided water to the gardens surrounding the small structure. Nothing decorative graced the stone-veneered walls. None of the Sisters could be seen.

Angeline's 'find' spell indicated De Spar had not left the shrine. She loosened the sword belted at her waist. Her baggy trousers, soft leather shirt, and supple knee-high boots would allow her freedom of movement if it came to sticking the pointy end of her weapon into the enemy. She smiled at the phrase. It was the first lesson Malcolm had taught her when they had begun sparring.

"Are we going to dash in and surprise him?" asked Conner.

A figure exited the shrine. From a distance it looked like a penguin, the small creatures that inhabited the frozen reaches of the Central Land's inhospitable southern border. With a flash, it disappeared from the doorstep and materialized a handful of arm length's away.

"Apparently not," said Angeline.

The creature was only slightly taller than Conner. His ebony eyes with flames for irises proclaimed him demonic. Dressed as a manservant, black trousers and tight jacket with tails, bright white shirt with starched, wing-tipped collar, De Spar's emissary held a silver charger before him. Upon it lay a folded sheet of parchment. He walked up to Angeline and gave her a head bow.

"Lady Simon. I bring an invitation from my master." He offered the charger. Angeline picked up the paper and opened it. The manservant continued, "Your betrothed is well, though he appears to be in a foul mood."

"Fowl?" said Conner. "Did the demon turn your betrothed into a bird?"

"Hush, fool," Angeline said to Conner. She dropped the invitation back on the charger. "Tell your master, De Spar, we would be happy to discuss the matter."

The manservant disappeared. The scent of cinnamon lingered.

He's overconfident. We've got him. She looked at Conner. "We've been invited into the shrine to negotiate Malcolm's release."

"It's a trap, Mistress."

"Of course it is, but surprise was never a possibility. Now we don't have to fight our way in. Half the battle is won."

"It's the other half I worry about, Mistress."

"What's your point?" retorted Angeline. Conner's negativism grated her nerves. "This demon thinks he's already defeated us. We have him where we want him. Malcolm's as good as free." She snapped her fingers for emphasis. "Think it, and it's done. Come along."

Angeline's magical senses tingled as soon as she entered the apse. *Glamour.* Her eyes were drawn to the human dressed in an elegant white shadow, tone on tone, vested pinstripe. *De Spar.* Dark hair slicked back, amazingly deep cobalt eyes which Angeline swore could read her very soul, and alabaster hands folded in his lap, gave the impression of the well-to-do, not a devotee to a goddess. Only his blue, green, and white paisley ascot seemed out of place. His manservant stood by his side.

Angeline tore her gaze away from the demon and looked around. In place of the altar, which replaced the gristmill taken by the previous occupants, sat an overstuffed wingback chair. The footing depicted cloven hooves while the rolled arms sported knuckled handholds in the form of taloned claws.

Far from light and airy, the oak paneling and exposed iron wood beams gave the room a dark and somber tone, almost cave-like. Before the wingback, two armless wingback chairs waited.

"Please be seated," said De Spar. A teapot and a decanter appeared on his manservant's charger. "Would you like some tea or wine?"

Conner raised his hand. "I would like some—"

"No, you wouldn't," Angeline corrected. She wasn't about to give the demon an opportunity to drug them. She gave De Spar a slight head bow. "We're fine, thank you."

"As you will," said De Spar. He lifted a crystal goblet filled halfway with a red liquid that smelled of dark cherries, wet leaves, and a hint of copper. "I would like to thank you for agreeing to this visit. It saves unnecessary bloodshed. Shall we begin?"

Angeline looked over at Conner. She stuck her nose in the air and looked away, giving him her best "I-told-you-so" gesture. Angeline doubted the demon would keep his word but talking would give her an idea of how he thought. "Yes, let's. How is Malcolm? Can I see him?"

"That might be counter-productive." De Spar took a small sip of the wine. "He is alive and wishes to remain that way. Whether or not his wishes are fulfilled is up to you."

His soothing voice relaxed Angeline's fears or would have, but for his words which she found alarming. "If you've tortured him, there is no deal. I will not pay for damaged goods."

"What is torture? A little pain? A little discomfort? True, persuasion is not always pleasant, but sometimes torture is rapturous."

Deep down, De Spar's dulcet tones tingled parts of her she'd rather not mention. Her lips parted. *What was it that he had said?* "So, you are gently stroking Malcolm?"

"Why speak of this Malcolm?"

Angeline shivered. A warmth spread through her. Her tongue peeked out between her lips. She said huskily, "Who would you rather speak of?"

De Spar smiled. His eyes danced hypnotically. "You, Angeline. Yes, I know your name. That and much more. I know what to touch and when. I would take you with me back to the Lair. I would make you deliriously happy. Agree and I will let this Malcolm go. Refuse, and he will die."

The demon's last words triggered Angeline's awareness. *Spell of beguilement!* Awareness alone didn't help Angeline. She needed freedom of action. Intentionally languorous, Angeline reached up and stroked her pendant. Her brain fog lifted. She glanced at Conner and winked.

Branches sprang from De Spar's chair, securing his arms and legs. Before the wine glass hit the ground, Conner launched a fusillade of arrows and stones. The first arrow took the manservant between the eyes, the rest centered on De Spar's neck scarf. Sparks flew where Conner's weapons bounced off the demon.

De Spar bulged his muscles. The branches holding him snapped. He leaped out of the chair.

Angeline took a step back, aghast. Iron oak was the hardest wood in the Central Lands.

De Spar hefted an over-sized scimitar, heavier than a man his size should have been able to lift, as if it were a mere twig. "You would do this to me?" said De Spar with a hurtful voice. "After what I offered you? That is most unfortunate. But first, I'll deal with your nuisance pet."

Angeline searched through her knowledge of spells. Normally gifted with rapid recall, De Spar's pressure prevented her mind from grasping even basic concepts.

De Spar reached out his left hand. His magic lifted Conner from the ground.

A hand full of arrows appeared in the Reek's hand.

The demon closed his fingers, drawing Conner closer to De Spar.

The Easterner fired continuously, until he hung suspended before the demon's face.

"What's this? A puny human?" He sniffed. His eyes blazed. "Easterner!"

A greenish gas enveloped De Spar's face. The demon flung Conner out of the cloud with a thunderous bellow, "A Reek!"

The glamour disguising the shrine dissipated. De Spar frantically waved his free hand in front of his face to dispel the gas.

Angeline seized the moment. An air-tight bubble, containing much of the gas excreted by Conner, materialized around De Spar's head. The rest drifted toward Angeline. Conner hit the floor and rolled to his feet.

"Mistress, he called, "don't breathe the gas."

The warning came too late. Not even at her father's slaughter house had she ever smelt such a putrid stench. Her eyes watered. Her stomach roiled.

De Spar transformed into a huge red gargoyle, twice Angeline's size. Angry eyes, blazing like red-hot coals embedded in the darkest ebony, sent waves of horror through the young sorceress.

She wanted to flee. Involuntarily, she splayed her arms behind her so she wouldn't trip as she backed up a few steps.

De Spar, extended his arm to the side.

Malcolm appeared, suspended in the air next to the demon and encased in a shell like the one still around De Spar's head. Her betrothed, mouth open and gasping as his hands frantically probed the walls of the shell, desperately sought escape.

Angeline stopped and took a step forward. *A mirror spell!* Her legs went wobbly. Whatever she cast against De Spar would now also affect Malcolm. Her betrothed fell to his knees, hands reaching for his throat. As she watched, he slumped to the bottom of his shell.

Angeline cancelled her spell. The bubble around De Spar's head disappeared as did Malcolm's. He fell to the ground with a thud. Conner dashed to him and pulled him off to the side.

De Spar thrust back his shoulders and spread his leathery wings. They reached to the exposed rafters of the humble hermitage. He roared in outrage. The entire room shook with the force of his voice. Dust drifted down from the ceiling. The demon lunged forward.

Angeline fell back. De Spar's taloned fist blurred before her. The generated breeze caressed her face. There was no time for relief as Angeline felt a tug against the back of her neck and heard the snap of a chain. *No!* Her hand flew to her cylinder of Ambrosia. It was gone. Her pulse quickened. Her eyes darted about, finally locating the cylinder as it clattered across the wood floor.

De Spar grabbed again, this time snatching Angeline around the waist. He drew her close. "Aha! I have you. My goddess, Mieze, warned that you had a lot of promise," sneered De Spar. "But what you needed was ability!"

Angeline struggled. Contact with the demon drained her will. Soon she wouldn't have enough left to cast a spell. She cursed herself for falling into De Spar's grasp.

"You can take him, Mistress," said Conner. "You've got him right where you want him."

When I get out this, I'm going to throttle me a Reek, she promised herself. She glanced at Conner. He kept reaching for his neck and pointing to De Spar. *What's that idiot saying?* She didn't have time for charades. She had to get De Spar to release her.

Angeline didn't believe she could entice De Spar into freeing her with beguilement, but maybe if she went the other way? Gathering her failing strength, she drew on her own situation. The air in the room became heavy and burdensome. Misery and hopelessness made breathing difficult.

The fire in De Spar's eyes dimmed.

Angeline put every remaining ounce of will she had into her spell. Her voice quavered. It took on the timbre of doom and despair. "No one respects you. No one likes you."

His wings drooped.

It's working. Angeline inserted a little hope into her voice. "Release me and I will be your friend."

Mocking laughter burned her ears. De Spar's grip tightened as he stood tall. His grip continued to drain her will. "You have no power over me. You're just a child."

Angeline burned with humiliation. Her first big test and she was getting beaten, badly. An image of Doirbhall materialized in her mind. The healer ground something in her pestle. Angeline bristled. *Don't I have enough humiliation without you rubbing my nose in it?*

The enticing scent of Ambrosia wafted from the healer's image. Angeline recalled its hypnotic effect on her. *Of course!* If her arm were free of the demon's touch, perhaps she could gather enough will to compel the cylinder to her.

Squirm as she might, she couldn't get her arm free of De Spar's fist. Strength failing, frustration got the better of her. She snapped, "You wouldn't say that if I gave you the nectar of the gods!"

An immediate metamorphic change occurred in De Spar. "Ambrosia? You have Ambrosia?"

His huge scimitar clattered to the floor. His grip slackened.

She wrenched her arm out of De Spar's grasp. The breaking of contact brought Angeline a surge of will. She reached out her hand. "To me." The cylinder flew into her hand as if shot from a bow.

De Spar watched with interest, his forked tongue wetting then rewetting his lips.

A momentary pang of regret assailed Angeline. It wouldn't look good using her life saver in her first fight. *But neither would dying.* She waved her cylinder enticingly in front of the demon. "Guess what's in here?"

De Spar's focus centered entirely on the cylinder. His eyes followed its every movement. "Ambrosia?" he repeated. "For De Spar?"

Angeline unscrewed the cylinder. Honeyed scent tickled her nostrils. She felt invigorated. "Release me."

All remaining traces of De Spar's demonic personality vanished. His once blazing orbs now shone with a desire to please. He dropped to his knees and gently set her feet on the floor. He then sat back on his haunches looking like a puppy sitting before its master waiting for the slightest indication to play.

Angeline knew what she had to do and did not feel the least bit guilty. She inhaled the deeply of the aroma then held it out. "Yes, for De Spar."

De Spar reached for the rare treat.

Angeline pulled the cylinder back. "First you must take off your neck shield."

Without hesitation, De spar ripped the metal shield from his neck. It clattered as it bounced on the wood floor.

His ready compliance came as a shock to Angeline. *It must be the ground stone Doirbhall added to it.*

Underneath the shield, the skin of De Spar's neck pulsed. Little more than a membrane, it would offer little resistance to her sword. Angeline handed him the cylinder and drew her sword.

His sinuous tongue eagerly scooped the Ambrosia out of the cylinder. His eyes rolled back in ecstasy.

Angeline drove her sword through the thin membrane of his throat.

With a gurgling sound, De Spar's huge body dissolved.

"You did it, Mistress!" shouted Conner.

Angeline's weapon fell from nerveless fingers. She rushed toward Malcolm. Placing her hand over his chest, she searched for a heartbeat. She threw her head back, extending her senses to her fingertips. Nothing. "Beat," she commanded. Angeline fought back against her panic. She concentrated on Malcolm. "Beat. Tierra, help him, help me. Beat!"

Malcolm's chest convulsed. A thin reedy heartbeat pulsed beneath her fingers. It gained strength and settled into a regular rhythm.

Angeline exhaled slowly. Relief filled her. She whispered, "Thank you, Tierra, for Malcolm, and for keeping us alive."

Conner crept closer. He chewed his lower lip while wringing his hands. "Your betrothed? He lives?"

Angeline smiled. "He lives, Conner. We did it."

The Reek squatted down. He clasped his hands across his breast. His face glowed. "You proved your worth. It's so romantic."

Angeline sat up, basking in the adulation. She adopted an attitude. "Of course! I have ...," Angeline stopped her boast mid-sentence. She put her arm around Conner's shoulder and squeezed, "a lot more to learn."

81

An Act of Kindness

Space travel is tedious, thought Oguy. *Especially traveling with Yagg.*

Simply put, Yagg was an asshole. Oguy considered that quite an achievement since insectoids lacked that particular body part and, in all the known universe, achievement and Yagg did not simultaneously exist. To make matters worse, Yagg firmly believed the universe revolved around him.

Yagg's going to get his.

Oguy clung to that precept. In fact, he wanted to be there when it happened. Even better, he dreamed of being the one to deliver Yagg's comeuppance.

Oguy's eye cluster detected rapid movement. He ducked, but not in time to avoid the clout between his secondary eye and antennae. Yagg had entered the bridge and said hello. Oguy added the greeting to Yagg's ever-growing payback list.

"O goo eey," Yagg drawled, distorting the pronunciation of his shipmate's name. "Your reflexes are getting as slow as your metasoma is getting fat."

Yagg clacked his mandibles. Yagg always clacked his mandibles at his own jokes. No one else thought he was funny.

Oguy cleaned his feeler and checked it for damage. He mewled, "You're going to hurt someone one day. Or put some eyes out."

"Not someone with as hard an exo as you. It's positively dense and you have plenty of eyes," said Yagg. "Now, get up. You're sitting in my chair."

"Sorry," mumbled Oguy.

It didn't matter which of the two chairs he sat in. Yagg always wanted the one Oguy occupied. Oguy moved over.

As Yagg settled in, he asked, "Where are we going?"

"Sol system."

"Oh, them," said Yagg. "What level?"

"Level Five."

Yagg clacked his mandibles. His eye clusters lit up. "Extermination. My favorite. It couldn't happen to a more deserving race. They're totally worthless."

"You would know," said Oguy under his breath.

"What's that?"

"I said 'I think it's going to snow.'"

"There's no way it's going to snow. Man, you suck as a meteorologist."

Oguy ignored Yagg and thought instead of the target. The inhabitants of the planet slated for extinction had proven to be a huge disappointment. They simply couldn't get along. Like Oguy's tolerance of Yagg, the Queen and her council had been long-suffering of the humans, but one defective trait kept resurfacing. None of the inhabitants wanted to be equal, they either dominated or submitted. This time they would all submit. It would be their final act and the only one they ever did as a single race.

Oguy waved his feelers in Yagg's direction, "We're ready to jump."

Yagg input the coordinates Oguy activated his hive collar, the device through which the space-faring ants communicated long distance. He contacted Interstellar Control.

"Control Charlie Kilo, Element Foxtrot Uniform One Zebra Three, ready for jump."

"Foxtrot Uniform One Zebra Three, Control Charlie Kilo, roger, have you verified your coordinates?"

Oguy glanced in Yagg's direction. His partner excreted pheromones of agitation.

"Of course, they're good," said Yagg.

"That's affirmative, Control."

"Roger that. Foxtrot Uniform One Zebra Three, jump approved. Good Luck, you'll need it."

"Foxtrot Uniform."

"Charlie Kilo."

"What's that jerk's problem?" asked Yagg.

Oguy shot a look at Yagg's coordinates. He exhaled, his breath passing through the many holes in his exoskeleton, the equivalent of an insectoid sigh. "Beats me."

Their small interstellar craft leapt through the infinity of space, reappearing moments later in the middle of an asteroid belt. Yagg threw himself backwards against his seat. He raised four of his six arms up in front of him to shield himself from the rapidly approaching asteroids.

Calmly, Oguy maneuvered the craft away from the nearest space rock.

Yagg came out of his fright long enough to throw a back-hand in Oguy's direction. "What did you do?"

Oguy ducked away. "I'm sorry." He continued to dodge and weave through the worst of the field, adeptly avoiding the debris. "But I might remind you that you input the coordinates."

Yagg spun his chair to face Oguy. "Are you suggesting that this is *my* fault?"

Oguy maneuvered around a few more asteroids before finding a calm spot to merge with the field. He slumped back in his chair. It took all his willpower not to excrete pheromones of accusation. "You input the coordinates and verified them. That's all I'm saying."

"You must have jostled my claw," said Yagg, arranging himself more comfortably.

"I must have." Oguy looked away. He muttered under his breath, "You will never admit to anything."

"What's that?"

"I said 'I'm so happy I could sing.'"

"Spare me, your voice sucks."

"I'll report in." Oguy activated his hive collar. "Control Charlie Kilo, Element Foxtrot Uniform One Zebra Three."

"Element Foxtrot Uniform One Zebra Three, Control Charlie Kilo. You made it."

Oguy's feelers could almost smell the scent of surprise from Mission Control. "Affirmative."

"Standby for mission download."

"Foxtrot Uniform standing by," said Oguy. A moment later he added, "Receiving download. Download complete. Thanks Control. Foxtrot Uniform."

"Charlie Kilo."

"Uniform," added Yagg, clacking his mandibles and cutting the contact.

"You're not funny," said Oguy.

"He is. Funny looking, that is," said Yagg. ""What's the status?"

It wasn't good, not if you lived on the targeted planet. Oguy could relate to the inhabitants. Like his partnership with Yagg, they had originally been an experiment. Could a civilization exist without a hive mentality? Could they thrive? The DNA of the new race had been programmed for a high degree of independence. After forty thousand years, it appeared that they had too much.

All their 'independence' had led to selfishness. Nothing or no one mattered but themselves, individually. The Queen's decree declared that pattern of thought as having "no place in the universe."

Oguy studied Yagg out the corner of his eyes. He reviewed the mission download on his private scanner before finally answering Yagg's question about the status. "It's a go."

Yagg clacked his mandibles together. "This is my favorite part. How does She want us to do it?"

"Asteroid strike," said Oguy. "But just big enough to depopulate. The Queen intends to reseed the planet with proper life forms."

"Yeah, yeah, right. I'll take care of it."

"Okay. I got some down time, I think I'll take it. Remember, not a planet killer."

"Heh, heh. These snowflakes are going to have their feelings hurt real good. It serves them right. I think I'll target their safe space."

Oguy smiled, at least as much as insectoids could. He knew he had a little time before Yagg decided he wanted his own down time instead of allowing Oguy any. Oguy stopped by the storage locker. From there, he secured a half-kilo of diatomaceous earth and several pairs of gloves, which he took to Yagg's cocoon.

Oguy handled the specially wrapped package very carefully as he coated the inside Yagg's personal safe space with half of the fine powder. The abrasive and physico-sorptive properties of the diatomaceous earth would break down the waxy lipids that covered Yagg's exoskeleton. He would slowly dehydrate.

Oguy hummed a popular tune from his home world, "It Couldn't Happen to a Nicer Ant." He put the rest of the powder in the cocoon's breathing tank before disposing of the evidence. Yagg breezed into the compartment.

"Hey, slacker, I realized that it's my turn for down time. Get outta here and get back to work."

Oguy said nothing as Yagg positioned himself within his cocoon. Once it sealed, Oguy deactivated the emergency override, locking Yagg inside with no way of escape. He looked in on his partner.

Yagg squirmed around, trying to scratch his exoskeleton, but the close confines of the cocoon did not allow for enough movement. His eyes linked with Oguy's. "You miserable insect! You put itch powder in my cocoon. When I get outta here, I'm going to rip your feelers off. I'll tear your legs off one at a time. I'll—"

Yagg's voice cut off abruptly as Oguy held up the label of his special package.

"You'll do nothing to me ever again, Yagg."

Oguy adhered the label to the view port where Yagg would see it until the end. He then returned to the spacecraft's bridge. Yagg had, of course, selected too large a rock and aimed it at a volcanic caldera. Oguy shook his head. He hummed another tune, "Just Rewards" and made the necessary corrections. The two drones Yagg had dispatched earlier changed course. They weaved their way through the field to a smaller asteroid. One of the drones would nudge the rock out of the Kuiper belt and the other would fine-tune the trajectory toward the third planet, the blue one.

Oguy waited until the drones secured themselves to the selected asteroid then detonated the charge. The small asteroid left the belt on a perfect course.

"Control Charlie Kilo, Element Foxtrot Uniform One Zebra Three, over."

"Element Foxtrot Uniform One Zebra Three, Control Charlie Kilo, over."

"Mission accomplished, Control. Request permission to return to base."

"Both missions, Foxtrot Uniform?"

"Both missions, Control."

"The Queen will be pleased. Yagg was, how did She put it? An asshole."

Oguy clacked his mandibles.

THANK YOU FOR PURCHASING this book. If you have enjoyed these stories, check out other books by Bill Eckel.

Shem's Quest - Shem always wanted to be a hero — until he became one. Follow Shem as he quests to raise the Hjerte, the Heartstone, and secure Tierra's rising. Signed copies available through Billeckel.com

Hard Kill - Eliminate the Fleshies! Transhumanist ruled the dwarf-planet Eris. They have issued Hard Kill procedures to reduce the population. The Henry's want to live. To do so, they must reach the surface, alive.

Cadet Adam - Adam wants to save his cribbie, Evie who has joined the Psychic Wing while in the space academy. To do so, he must stop the Psychics plan to usurp the throne of the Ancient of Days, leader of the Most High Federation of Planets.

BILL ECKEL

An excerpt from Cadet Adam

LUC

Celeste, home planet of the Most High federation of planets, was under attack. To those enjoying the pleasant Spring morning in En-lil, the capitol city, the danger was not readily apparent. The ruling triumvirate, currently in session, was about to find out different.

Over-Lieutenant Luc looked up at the inscription chiseled in the granite lintel above the door of the Hall of Justice. 'The Truth shall set you Free.' He smirked. "And I shall enslave you. That is the truth."

Luc entered. Inside the Hall, He was led to the central chamber. Within sat the Triumvirate, those responsible for the governance of Celeste. Luc extended his senses. His astral projection considered his target. Premier Uta, the leading figure of Celeste's ruling council and long rumored to be the number three man in the Most High, was the one Luc needed. Like Luc, Uta was ambitious. Many ambitious men were easily directed. The other two, Anlon, Senior Departmental Head of the Government Corps, and Mira, Pastoral Shepherd of the Department of Faith, were mere bureaucrats, chattel to be disposed of. Luc returned to his body as the attendant-in-waiting opened the doors to the Hall of Justice and announced him.

At two meters, seventy, Luc was tall for a Celestial and possessed a breath-catching beauty, especially in the metallic sheen of his Fleet uniform. He immediately drew and held the attention of the Triumvirate as he entered. Their eyes followed his every movement as he strode to the podium before them. He sensed interest in Uta, the irritation of Anlon, and the visceral twinges of Mira reacting to his beauty. As the three rulers stared, he launched his attack.

"Honored rulers, a psychic menace spreads across the Most High. People are being born with psychic powers. Unknown and unchecked, it is capable of great evil. I have come to offer my assistance to the Ancient of Days in the harnessing of this phenomena."

Uta, Anlon, and Mira exchanged glances. Luc could sense the confusion and doubt they felt. Confident in his assessment of Uta, Luc slipped into the eververse, the psychic space between thought and reality. He located Uta's mental signature and delicately established a telepathic link. He stood ready to shut down Uta's motor controls if necessary. In a tone designed to soothe Uta's concerns, Luc sent, <Premier Uta, do not speak. Think, and I will hear.>

<You are one of them?>

<Not one, *the* one. I am the leader.>

<What do you want?>

<To give you a demonstration and offer a proposition.>

Uta paused.

Luc prepared to block off both of Premier Uta's carotid arteries, which would bring on a massive stroke. Luc was impressed by the fact the Premier kept such a tight control over his emotions. He could not sense which way Uta was leaning.

Finally, the Premier answered. <Proceed.>

Luc carefully concealed his satisfaction from his telepathic sending. <It would be mutually beneficial if you were to turn off the recording devices.>

The Premier was a savvy political veteran. He shifted his gaze from Mira and Anlon to Luc. His expression gave no indication of the surprise he felt, but this time Luc could feel it through the psychic link.

Luc let a sparkle appear in his eyes. He allowed the corners of his mouth to turn up for the fleeting moment during the assessment he knew Uta was giving him. Uta's hand drifted to his slate-comp. His fingers moved.

Round one to me. Luc enjoyed the pleasurable thought.

Anlon was the first to verbally respond. "Uta, who let this man in here?" His voice was tainted with pompous bureaucratic belligerence. "Who are you, Over-Lieutenant?"

Uta remained silent. He kept his hands folded in front of him, seemingly more interested in Luc's response than answering Anlon's question.

Luc held a special contempt for bureaucrats. Their departments were ponderous, slow-moving, and rarely accomplished anything of worth. He considered those to be their good points. "Senior Department Head Anlon, I am Over-Lieutenant Luc, Fleet Officer of the Most High. I realize you have not heard of any menace. This is my initial report."

Anlon frowned as he formulated his next question. Mira, her voice soft-spoken and caring, beat him to it. "How extensive is this spread? And how is it *you* know of it?"

"Pastoral Shepherd—"

"I prefer Sister."

Luc turned on his charm. He knew his smile was dazzling. "Sister Mira, I can say for a certainty that there are psychics on Celeste, Saiph, Betelgeuse, and Tau Ceti e. Those are the only locations I have discovered so far. However, I have not visited the entirety of the Most High."

"You can tone down the visual display, Over-Lieutenant. I am only interested in the facts," said Mira.

Luc fumed inwardly. He was not used to rejection. He let his smile die and adopted a more neutral expression. "Of course, Sister."

Anlon addressed Uta. "I think he is either a kook or shyster."

"Afraid of competition?" chimed in Mira.

"Save your wit for your dimwitted flock, Mira," responded Anlon.

Uta asked, "Do you believe him, Mira?"

"He's wasting our time," interjected Anlon.

"Maybe," said Mira. "Maybe not. Our Maker is amazing." She sat forward. "What exactly has our Maker done with his people, Over-Lieutenant?"

Luc stopped his initial reaction to smile. He was not overtly religious, but he was not ignorant of the teachings. "Each according to their needs, Sister, and with what strength they can manage."

"I'll do the preaching, Over-Lieutenant. Please be specific."

Bitch, thought Luc. "Telepathy, astral projection, intuitive—"

Mira snorted, "You cannot just make these statements without proof."

"That's right, charlatan," Anlon added. "Words are meaningless."

Luc flicked a glance at Anlon. *You'll get yours.* He held out his hand toward Mira. "I'll need something of yours. Your hand-comp, perhaps."

She looked accusingly at Luc.

Luc shrugged. "Turn it off, first. It is not what is in it, merely that you have touched it."

Mira deactivated her device. As she took her hand away from it, it rose off the table to a height of seven centimeters. All six eyes of the Triumvirate followed its progress to Luc's open palm. He closed his hand around it.

When Luc first discovered his abilities, he had thought something was wrong with him. With time and increased skill, he realized that nothing was wrong. It was right. Images of Mira's young adult days living in the brothel section of En-lil played in Luc's mind. He smiled. "Six in one day. You were a hard worker."

She managed to suppress her shock and embarrassment from the Triumvirate, but not Luc. "I've heard enough."

Anlon looked between Mira and Luc. "What? What does that mean?"

Mira leaned back in her chair. She studied Luc with cold, calculating eyes. "I believe him, Premier. Look at him. He is too smug to be lying. He is right and he knows it."

Premier Uta steepled his fingers. Discussion stopped. "Over-Lieutenant, why did you use the term 'menace' to describe these psychics?"

Luc kept his expression neutral. Inwardly, he rejoiced. The Premier had just asked for the demonstration Luc alluded to earlier. He was more than happy to oblige. He chose Anlon's mind. The fool was broadcasting his feelings freely and he was irritating. Luc matched Anlon's alpha waves and went right in. Once inside, he went directly to the medulla oblongata and stimulated it to increase the blood flow to the brain. An aneurysm rapidly developed in Anlon's basilar artery.

The bureaucrat grasped his temples in obvious pain. He squeezed his eyes shut. The aneurysm in his head burst, killing him instantly. He fell forward, his head landing on the table before him.

Blood trickled out of Anlon's ears and the corner of his mouth. Uta raised an eyebrow. His voice was expressionless. "What happened to him?"

Luc matched the Premier's tone. "Aneurysm."

Mira's eyes widened as she grasped what had just happened. "You did that?"

Luc turned his icy gaze on Mira. "Yes, Sister. I did."

Her breath came in quick gasps. Her eyes flicked back and forth between Luc and Uta. "Why?"

Luc stared at Uta. "I believe the Most High would benefit from a different Ancient of Days. One that knew the usefulness of a changing society. Don't you?"

Uta nodded. "I could see the benefit of change."

Don't miss out!

Visit the website below and you can sign up to receive emails whenever Bill Eckel publishes a new book. There's no charge and no obligation.

https://books2read.com/r/B-A-IKDV-MRQJC

BOOKS 2 READ

Connecting independent readers to independent writers.